PETER LINGARD

THE BOOK OF

Every number tells a story

This is a work of fiction. Names, characters and events are the products of the author's imagination. Any resemblance to actual persons, living or dead, or actual events is purely coincidental.

First Published 2019

National Library of Australia Cataloguing-in-Publication entry:
Creator: Lingard, Peter author.
Title: The Book of Dave, Peter Lingard.
ISBN: 978-0-6483273-5-6 (paperback)

Cover design by Cathy Larsen (cathylarsendesign.com)
Tale Publishing
Melbourne Victoria

Contents

Prologue

1995

Barman Dave Wilson took his mandated fifteen minute break from his party laden shift on the twenty-eighth of December and picked up a pen and one of the 1996 diaries/address books the pub offered its customers. He perched on a stool at the end of the bar and pulled the well-worn 1995 diary from his back pocket and extracted a number of papers. After unfolding them, he ironed them with the edge of his hand. That done, he had a collection of variously hued notes of differing textures. The stack included a number of business cards, neat white memo squares, betting slips, two torn corners of newspapers, a bandage wrapper and a yellow 'stick 'um'. There was a page ripped from an address book, another from a ruled note book, a scrap of wrapping paper, a piece of a paper napkin, and part of a cigarette packet. The pile grew with a piece of what must have been a menu ('onsome' above 'uck L'orange'), a pink tissue, an oblong of pale blue personalised note paper, a shred of toilet paper, and a five pound note bearing the mark of a red kiss and a telephone number written in lipstick. 'I don't remember this,' he murmured and put the money in his wallet. 'I wonder if the fiver was hers or mine.' His fifteen minutes spent, he decided to take the papers home, sift through them without distraction. As he was currently suffering from writers' block, his writing hobby could wait while he recorded those details he wanted to retain into the new the address book.

Let Me Entertain You

As he wasn't due at work until five-thirty the next evening, Dave started to sort through the papers as soon as he finished his breakfast. At the top of his pile lay the homemade business card of the pub's cellar man. He'd given it to Dave in case someone needed a deejay. Bert, the middle-aged Geordie, managed the cellar and acted as a security escort whenever the landlord took the previous day's takings to the bank.

The balding man was the pub's deejay on 'Karaoke Nights'. His wife, Deirdre took request slips, led the singing, and persuaded nervous vocalists to step up to the microphone. Whenever Bert chose music to attract the under-thirties crowd, many clients had to be 'proofed', as refusals to serve those thought to be underage sometimes resulted in ugly scenes. Many young women hated the taste of alcohol and added sweet soft drinks to make it palatable. They then often drank too much and some were physically sick in the bathrooms and on the pavement outside the pub. Others fell asleep on their seats or stared intently at the carpet pattern in an attempt to steady their dizzy heads. Bert's first job in the morning was to clean the pub's walls, the car park, and the pavements around two sides of the pub.

Young men tried to impress young women (and themselves) by gulping shots of whisky with beer chasers. Some then helped decorate the exterior walls of the pub. As the night progressed, talk at the bar turned to imagined deeds of heroic violence, before males started to scout the room for lucky females. Others formed groups and headed to clubs or impromptu parties. Desperate loners backed up their drinks as they fought oblivion, sometimes leaving three or four untouched drinks on tables after closing time.

Bert and Deirdre also provided suitable music for theme nights which brought in an older crowd. Prizes were awarded for the best costumes. Women took the occasions more seriously than the men, especially if the theme called for costumes that pushed jellied breasts up, out, and into everyone's face. 'Vicars and Tarts' was always popular, as was 'Gone with the Wind', and 'Pirates of Penzance'. Most husbands and boyfriends were reluctant to dress up, but there were men who loved to don a frock. Half-a-dozen regulars, all friends, wore dresses at every opportunity, using mop-heads for wigs and balloons for breasts. When dancing, they hiked their dresses to show their hairy legs. They were boisterous, fun-loving characters who often led the singing and dancing. Everyone wore a smile when the 'sexy six' were in form.

Dave knew he might want to contact Bert at odd hours, plus if he found the man a deejaying gig he could charge him a fee. He entered Bert's number in his new diary and put his card in the wallet-like space at the back cover.

PUFF

A group of people who appeared to be 'out on the town' gathered at the pub one Friday night. Amongst them was a stunning woman whose shiny, light-brown hair curled on her shoulders. She had challenging hazel eyes under thick eyebrows, and, left of her chin, a mole that doubled as a beauty mark. Dave had been fascinated by her full, purple-painted lips. Unlike other women in the group, the stunner stood and matched the men drink for drink and joke for joke. She wore a charcoal-grey pin-stripe suit and a white lace blouse, the top button of which she unfastened after her second Absolut and soda, revealing a glimpse of tanned cleavage. The businesswoman's shapely legs were sheathed in grey stockings with a black seam and she wore black patent leather shoes on exceptionally high heels. Dave had never seen tights with a seam, so he assumed that, under the medium-length skirt, the woman wore suspenders to hold up thigh-high stockings.

It wasn't long before she came to the bar. 'Same again, please,' she ordered.

'I need some help with what the same is,' Dave told her.

'Oh, really? I was hoping you'd know.' She ran her tongue between her lips, making them glisten fetchingly and used one hand to count fingers on the other. She gave up. 'Hang on, I'll have to ask. Pour me an Absolut on the rocks with a twist to keep me going, will you?'

'My pleasure.' Dave dragged a glass through the bucket of ice and packed the small cubes tightly. He grabbed the bottle of vodka and flipped it over in the air before pouring the slightly viscous liquid. He held the bottle well above the glass, hoping the woman would return and witness the impressive stream of liquid splashing onto the icy rocks. Unfortunately, she was still checking on the order as the stream dwindled to a dribble.

Details obtained, the woman returned to the bar. Dave watched her hips roll. He picked out a medium-sized piece of lemon-rind and twisted it into a bow, forcing its zest to squirt down into the drink. He then bent the spent fruit on the rim of the glass.

'On me,' he said as he placed the drink in front of her.

'Thank you.' She rewarded him with a warm smile. 'Now, I need two pints of best bitter, a scotch and ice, a pint of Guinness…'

Dave interrupted her. 'Can I give you a tip?'

'Please do,' the looker said, slightly put out.

'Always order the Guinness first. It takes time to pour the stuff properly and other drinks can be made whilst the stout settles.'

'Oh, okay. I'll remember that. Thanks.'

'Now, what kind of scotch and what else do you need?'

'Oh, I've no idea about the scotch. Just give me whatever good stuff is popular these days. I'll also need a gin and tonic, a white Zinfandel, a dry sherry and a Coke with lots of ice.'

'I'll give you Famous Grouse and our Coke is Pepsi, is that all right?'

'Who cares? Are you always so particular?'

'I am when it comes to cola. They get a little irritated if they discover anyone serving the other brand as theirs. We have to point out that we serve Pepsi, not Coke.'

The woman smiled again. 'The things you learn!'

~

Later, as Dave watched the woman, he saw her flip the lapel of her suit jacket to reveal a small, gold-and-silver badge. The man she faced stopped talking, put down his drink, and unzipped his fly.

Dave readied himself for a confrontation. The rest of the group roared with laughter and applauded as the man put his hand inside his trousers and then withdrew it to reveal pink underpants gripped between thumb and forefinger. Other drinkers in the bar stopped what they were doing and turned to see if the man was about to pull anything else out of his pants. Dave quickly started toward the gate that would allow him access to the public side of the bar. The pullee paused, grinned, and then closed the gap in the material. Dave exhaled and relaxed. Once reassembled, the man made the businesswoman the flippee. Dave held his breath once more as she slowly unzipped her skirt. The quietening of the room highlighted every click of the slowly descending zipper. She spread the fabric and lifted the hem of her blouse to reveal a curvy hip encased in pink lace. Dave imagined he saw a hint of black suspenders. The crowd in the room whistled and applauded. The beauty zipped up her skirt, bent her knees, and spread her arms in a mock curtsy. Dave released his breath and looked for someone to serve.

'What was all that about?' He asked a man who purchased the next round of drinks for the group.

'That? Oh, we're all PUFFs,' the man said.

Dave didn't like the implication of the word. He swallowed his disappointment. 'PUFFs?'

'That's correct. We're all members of the Pink Underwear For Friday club. Anytime someone flashes the club badge at you on a Friday, you have to prove you are wearing pink underwear.'

Dave's hope rose again. 'Sounds like fun. Can anyone join?'

'Absolutely. Just have to pledge you'll wear pink underwear on Fridays and not hesitate to prove it whenever and wherever challenged.'

'I'm in.' Given he was trapped behind the bar, Dave felt that becoming a PUFF was the best way to get to know the sensual woman.

'Write down your name and address and give it to Sarah. Once you pay the dues and sign the pledge, she'll mail you a membership badge.'

'Which one is Sarah?'

'The woman standing up. She revealed her pink panties a few

minutes ago.'

Once the man had returned to the group with the last of the drinks, Dave waved Sarah to the bar and filled her in on his conversation with her fellow PUFF. He handed her a paper on which he'd written his required details.

'How soon before I can call myself a PUFF?'

She smiled. 'I can probably have the badge mailed to you by Wednesday or Thursday. Do you want to give me the club dues now, or wait until next Friday? I don't have a blank pledge with me, so we'll have to take care of it next week.'

'How much are the dues?'

'Twenty pounds per annum. Cash.'

Dave handed her the money, 'Where will you all be next Friday?'

'We don't know yet. We usually arrange matters during the week. I'll call you if you like and let you know.'

'With this job, you'll never know when I'll be around. Why don't you give me your number and I'll call you?'

Sarah looked at the paper Dave had given her, and seemingly thought about whether she wanted to give the barman her number. He waited while she assessed him, just as he'd assessed her. He weighed ninety-three kilos, stood a hundred-and-eighty-two centimetres, and was thirty-two years old. His days of playing semi-pro rugby had left him with bumps and scars he hoped women like Sarah found attractive.

A man sitting next to her, sipping his pint, and reading the sports section of the evening paper was surprised when she asked if she could tear off the top corner of the page. 'I have to give this man my number,' she said. He grinned with a look that could make a stranger believe he'd made the introductions. Sarah asked the also smiling barman for a pen.

~

Dave received his badge on Thursday and immediately called Sarah to thank her and to find out where they planned to meet the next day.

'At The Oar House in Henley. Do you know the place?'

'No, but I'll find it.'

'Are you working?' Sarah didn't give him the chance to reply.

'Get there early. As it's a long weekend, some of us will be there by three, or so. It's regatta time and we should have a lot of fun. See you then.'

~

Dave wondered where he could buy pink underpants. A tailor? Maybe, but he wasn't about to go that route. Carnaby Street, Camden Town market, Portobello Road, Kings Road, or Soho? He took the tube to Soho where he found a leather-and-chains store displaying shocking pink underwear with the caution 'Love me tender' emblazoned on the rear. He had to buy a packet containing three pairs for twelve pounds, but he was so desperate to get out of the store, he paid the sum without a murmur.

~

It hadn't occurred to Dave how people might react when asked for directions to The Oar House.

'I had no idea we had one in Henley,' said an attractive woman at the train station. 'I could provide the same services at my place free of charge,' she offered.

He smiled and paused before replying. 'Thanks, but actually it's a pub and I'm supposed to meet some people there.' The woman seemed to pretend embarrassment. 'A pub? Oh. Oh! Whatever must you think?'

'I think it's a great idea. If you give me your number, I'll call you another day.' (She had given him her number but he hadn't called her. He wondered if he would come across her details in his pile of papers.)

One man stated he had no idea where the place might be but swore he would remain rooted to the spot, if Dave promised to return once he found the place and could advise him of the address. A grey-haired woman clucked and walked away as if offended. Eventually Dave found an idle taxi driver who gave such a complicated routing that Dave hired the man to drive him to the pub.

Many club members were already in attendance and the obligatory newcomer's round was expensive.

Sarah asked him to sign the pledge and requested to see his badge. 'Just to make sure you're wearing it.' She grinned at him mischievously. Dave lifted his shirt collar to show the badge pinned underneath. 'Oh, you've got me!' The beautiful woman couldn't really pull off the mock surprise, but she did lift her halter to show she was wearing a skimpy pink bra with the badge attached. 'Your turn.'

Dave unzipped his fly and revealed his pink briefs. Thankfully, he didn't have to show the back side. His fellow PUFFs whistled, cheered and clapped their hands in appreciation.

Suddenly, one of his new-found friends called out. 'Look who's out there directing traffic! It's Timothy.'

'We have to flash him there at the cross-roads,' a laughing woman suggested.

'It's down to you then,' someone said.

PUFFs gathered at the windows overlooking the crossroads to watch the woman stride up to the busy policeman and flash her badge. The bluecoat stared at her in horror and said something they couldn't hear.

'Don't let him off the hook, Isabel," shouted a man in the group.

Isabel mouthed words back to Tim and, with arms akimbo, assumed a determined stance. The policeman raised his arms to halt the traffic from the North and East. He then repeated the manoeuvre to halt the traffic from the South and West. All vehicles stopped, he unzipped his fly and extracted a couple of inches of pink underpants. A driver got out of his car and applauded. A woman in another vehicle hid her face in her hands. Horns honked. Three spotty teenagers jeered. The PUFFs exited the pub and raised their glasses in salute.

'Atta boy, Tim.'

'Good show.'

'Once a PUFF always a PUFF!' caused the teenagers to convulse with laughter.

'What did he say to you?' a club member asked Isabel when she returned.

She was still laughing and had difficulty in getting the words out. 'He…he…he didn't b…believe I meant it. He…he screamed, "You can't be serious. I'm on duty here". When I said I was very serious, he cursed me. It was brilliant. A Bobby on traffic duty flashing pink underwear. It has to be a first.'

At four-twenty, a member named Harold instructed all PUFFs to follow him. He led them thirty metres down the road to where a stile in a fence allowed passage from road to river. A boat club stood across the road. Above the white garage-type doors a board bore the words, THE RIGHT ROYAL ROWERS.

'Unlike PUFFS, this isn't one of your snooty clubs,' Harold advised them as the doors opened and a line of men emerged, carrying an inverted shell over their heads.

'Hello, Colin,' roared Harold. 'We couldn't wait for you to join us, so we came to you.'

The front of the shell rose, affording the first man a view of Harold. 'Oh no, not now.'

'Can you see this badge, Colin?'

'Yes, Harold, I can.'

'And do you know what it means, Colin?'

'Yes, Harold, I do.'

Everyone cheered as Colin ordered the rest of the rowers to put down the shell. They lifted the craft, then turned and gently placed it on the ground. Colin unbuckled the white canvas belt around his waist, unzipped his fly and dropped his shorts. He put his right hand on his hip, lifted his left arm high in the air and executed a shuffling pirouette. His movement and an obliging breeze combined to ruffle his shirt and reveal pink trunks. His fellow oarsmen applauded the move, which Colin performed adroitly, considering his shorts were around his ankles.

'Bravo!'

'Well done!'

'Fine figure of a man.'

'Are these the new 'Triple 'R' colours?'

Colin reassembled his clothing and instructed his crew to pick up the shell. The team precariously traversed the stile and crossed the grass to the water. The PUFF's offer to fetch the oars was declined, so they returned to the pub.

~

In a quieter moment Dave asked Sarah, 'Can we have dinner together next week?'

'As in a date? No, Dave, we're fellow PUFFs, that's all.'

His whisky-loosened tongue flapped on. 'Look, I only joined this wacky club so I could get a date with you.'

'That was foolish of you. And I *do* hope you meant wacky in the fun sense of the word.'

'What? Yes, of course. Listen, you have to tell me something. Were you wearing suspenders last Friday?'

'Was I *what*?'

'I'm sorry. It's just that I was so turned on thinking you might be wearing suspenders. Were you?'

'Actually, I was. Unfortunately for you, I was wearing them for someone else's benefit. The blinkered fool was with me all day and didn't seem to notice.'

'Hey, I noticed. Doesn't that count for something?'

'Yes. It serves to demonstrate you're a horny bastard.'

'And you're not?'

She paused. A grin started at her mouth and grew in her eyes. 'Suppose I am. What of it?'

'Well, we could be horny together.' He raised his eyebrows.

'Just how horny are you, Dave?'

'So horny, the crack of dawn isn't safe! You?'

She laughed. 'Pretty much the same, 'though I can't match your symbolism. If we get together tonight, you have to understand it is only for tonight and that I have my sights set on a very different target. Understood?'

~

'That was one of the best night's I've had,' Dave told her the next morning. 'Can't you give up the chase of your blinkered target?'

'It was wonderful, Dave, but you agreed it was a one-off,' Sarah told him with a subdued smile. 'I'll grant you this. I'll keep your number in case my blinkered target is not really so blinkered.' A trace of sadness appeared in her eyes. 'Perhaps it's just that I'm not his type. If that realisation ever dawns, you'll be the first person I call.' Dave smiled but knew better than to say anything. 'One thing puzzles me,' Sarah said. 'Why did a worldly, heterosexual man such as you join a group of gay exhibitionists?'

Dave's blood rose with embarrassment. 'Gay?' he whispered.

'Of course! Who else would wear pink underpants? Where did you buy yours? Not at a regular clothing store, I'll bet.'

'I could ask you the same question.'

'I started the club amongst people I work with. We were just a regular group who got together every Friday to unwind. One of them, who unbeknown to me at the time is a gay man , asked if outsiders could join. Eventually, gay men became the largest percentage of our membership.'

'I told you. I just needed to get a date with you.'

The smile on Sarah's face was happy again. 'I knew you were straight. That was another reason I welcomed you; I hoped you'd help redress our disparity. But I must say, your sometimes rash behaviour needs curbing.'

He smiled. 'Well, that job's yours, whenever you want it.'

Dave smiled at the memory of Sarah. She never took him up on his job offer and consequently he had let his membership of PUFF lapse. The group had stopped using the pub as a rendezvous point and he wondered if Sarah had caused the change because of him. He reluctantly screwed up the corner of newspaper and lobbed it towards the waste bin, then he remembered the woman at the station and searched his papers for her number.

Horses for Courses

A torn commercial bookmark bore a message in purple nail polish. Dianne Lloyd. She'd told Dave she was getting a divorce and he should call her in a couple of months. How long ago was that? He remembered her well. She used to come into the pub with her husband and always wore low-cut tops. When she sat and rested her forearms on the bar, and he bothered to look between a couple of not so minor obstructions, he could see her belly button.

'She's trouble,' his blonde Irish co-worker Ellen had said.

Dave thought Ellen might be correct, but trouble could be fun. Since he'd realised how important Jane was to him, Dave hadn't dated another woman. However, he was reluctant to end to his annual routine. He no longer intended to sleep with any of them, so what harm could there be in keeping their numbers? If his relationship with Jane didn't work out, he would have details of women who wanted to get horizontal with him. He entered Dianne's number into the diary and threw away the bookmark.

A business card was next. 'Shit! This guy still owes me twenty quid!' He made a note in the 'appointments' section of the new diary.

Dave narrowed his eyes in concentration as he tried to recall who'd given him the number written on a page torn from a Filofax.

'If it was me dat gave yuh *me* number and yuh didn't call widdin tree days, I'd be pissed,' Ellen had once told him. 'You tink dese women give their numbers to anyone? For you tuh treat dair confidences so casually sucks. If yuh have no intention of calling dem, don't ask for deir numbers.'

He didn't always have to ask.

Sometimes, in the light of day, he had second thoughts. That, or, as in this case, he had no idea whose number it was. He threw the paper in the bin.

The bottom half of an unused cash invoice, a casual document used by people who dislike revealing their income to the taxman, bore a number written in pencil. The man's name was Edgar and he only ever ordered one drink per visit. However, he made seven or eight visits per day, six days per week. Dave knew Edgar worked at one of the antique stores in the vicinity. He came in at different times of the day for a measure of Famous Grouse. Dave wasn't sure of Edgar's sexual orientation but, on a whim, he had given him Sarah's phone number and told him about PUFF. If Edgar was gay the group might bring him happiness and if he wasn't, Sarah would be pleased. A month later, Edgar gave Dave the paper with his phone number written in pencil and told him, 'You ever need anything just let me know. Anything.'

Dave had assumed it was a way of thinking him for the PUFF contact details but, without more information, had not known how to react. 'Er, thanks, Ed.'

'Anything,' the man had repeated.

Sid Solomon's card was next. The man came into the pub to watch afternoon horse racing on television. The first time Dave noticed him had been during a race in which a horse trailing the field took a different course to the winning post. Dave had supposed the jockey was an idiot, or the horse had sustained an injury.

Sid had burst out laughing. 'Will ya look at that? The bleedin' fix must be in. That 'orse is the one on the right track. All de udders followed the big chestnut insteada takin' that left turn. Unfuckinbelievable!'

After each race, Sid would order a fresh drink, study the racing pages, then go to the turf accountant's shop across the road. He would return waving betting slips, settle on a barstool, and sip his gin and tonic. 'Gambling's me business,' he had informed Dave one day. 'Not this chicken-shit,' he'd said, nodding at the television. 'Cards; I play and I arrange. You ever get a punter in 'ere lookin' for some action, you give 'im me number.' He had produced a business card and passed it to Dave. On a couple of occasions, Sid had insisted the barman take a gamble on a particular horse and Dave had been pleased with the outcome.

He didn't think he'd be approached by anyone looking for an organised card game, but Dave entered the number in his new diary before ditching the dog-eared card.

A Fair Cop

Seven men aged from their late thirties to early fifties arrived at the pub for afternoon drinks. They gathered at the bar, looked the house over, and asked each other in broad Cockney accents if they had ever been in the place before. One of the men told Dave to serve everybody. Two wanted Johnnie Walker Black, one a Martels and Coke (the Coke/Pepsi routine was brushed aside with a 'Yeah, yeah, yeah. Tell me somefink I care abaht.'). Another ordered a pint of best bitter. A man with the broadest accent Dave had heard demanded a Winona. Dave had never heard of the drink.

'Do leave off! Ya call yourself a bleedin' barman and ya don't even know what a fuckin' Winona is. Why don't ya fuckin' find aht?'

'If you want to drink it, pal, you need to tell me what it is.'

He turned to a friend. ''E must be bleedin' stupid or somefink!'

Dave tired of the routine. 'What can I get *you*?' he asked the next man.

'A pinta tops.'

Dave put half-an-inch of lemonade in a glass and filled it up with bitter.

Meanwhile, the man who had asked for the 'Winona' was getting his mileage out of the situation. With his back to the bar, he addressed fellow drinkers. 'D'ya 'ear that? This fuckin' twat don't know what a fuckin' Winona is.' He laughed and his companions laughed with him.

'Listen friend,' Dave said to the back of the man's head. 'Firstly, you've got to clean up the language, and secondly I'll be happy to serve you your choice of drink if you'll just tell me exactly what it is you want.'

'Let it go, Fred. I 'ad no fuckin' idea what the shit was 'til ya told me. I fink ya made up the bleedin' name yerself.' The man who had spoken turned to Dave. 'Winona is Winona Ryder. Stupid prat wants a fuckin' pinta cider.'

'Thanks.' Dave pulled the pint of apples and put it on the bar in front of his antagonist.

'Give us a gee and tee wiv a twist,' said the man who had the air of the leader. 'Start a tab for us, will ya.' The 'will ya' was not meant to convey a question.

'I'll need your credit card.'

'Fuck off. I'll give it to ya when we leave.'

'Sorry, but I have to have a credit card now, or you can pay cash.'

'Listen to me, my son. I know the owner 'ere and I'm allowed to keep me credit card in me pocket 'til I settle the bleedin' bill at a time that's convenient ta me. Uvvawise any bleedin' prat could drink on me tab.'

'Look. I already asked you to watch the language. Now, if I don't get some cash or your credit card right now, I'll call the police. Anything else is more than my job is worth.'

'Don't be so bleedin' touchy, my son. Like I said, the owner is a mate a mine so you won't be losing any job 'ere. 'Im an' me go back a long ways.'

'Two points. I'm not your son and the owner here is a woman.'

The man was not fazed at being caught in a lie. 'A bleedin' woman! What kinda boozer is owned by a fuckin' skirt? An' what kinda fuckin' nonce are you, takin' orders from one?' The man turned to his friends, 'This 'ere arsehole finks he's gonna tell me what to do. I'll 'ave his bollocks in a fuckin' ringer.'

'The bill comes to eighteen pounds, thirty.' Dave told the man.

'Yeah, yeah. Later.'

Every customer watched the hostility. A couple left the pub; the squeaking of the door was the only sound to break the tense silence.

Dave was getting annoyed and nervous. 'I need the money or a credit card now.'

'Can't you get it frough your fick, fuckin' 'ead that you aint gettin' it,' snarled the man. Dave reached for the telephone.

A customer at the end of the bar walked over to the seven drinkers and flashed a police warrant card. 'Detective Sergeant Baxter. Do you know it's illegal to drink alcoholic beverages not paid for? It's to do with taxes and the like. Do you also know I could arrest you for the continued use of offensive language, especially after you've been asked to tone it down? I suggest you pay the man in cash right now and apologise to the other customers for your language.'

'I never 'eard no-one tell us to stop wiv the language. Anyhows, what's wrong wiv it? Don't tell me nobody in 'ere 'as never 'eard it all before.' Despite the man's truculent attitude, he placed a twenty-pound note on the bar.

'I'm sure everybody *has* heard it before. That doesn't mean they like it. Why don't you men finish your drinks and leave. By the way, I'll be calling the station house to let my colleagues know you lot are in the area. And what kind of nonce drinks something called a Winona?'

The cider man looked hard at the policeman and then at the group's apparent leader. He put his glass down on a table and took a menacing step towards the detective.

'Nah, Stevie, let it be. We don't wanna upset the local plods.'

Some of the men took a long time to finish their drinks, but the group eventually left without further trouble. After the cockneys had departed, Dave went to where the policeman sat.

'Thanks for your help. Can I get you a drink on the house?'

'No thanks. I might like this pub, so I'll be coming in regularly for a while. I'll pay for my drinks here – just to keep it all above board.'

'That doesn't mean I can't give you a free one by way of saying thanks, does it?'

'Okay. I'll have another Dewars. Thanks. My name's Frank, by the way.'

'Dave.' He wiped his hand on a cold, damp bar-rag before shaking the policeman's hand.

~

The cop did make the pub his local and he and Dave became friends. Other cops often joined him. They always congregated at the end of the bar where Frank had sat on his first day. Sometimes, when business was slow, Dave would chew on a toothpick and talk with the policeman.

'You know a number of bent guys are regulars here?' Frank asked one day.

'You mean bent sexually or criminally?'

'Criminally for the most part, although a couple of nonces do come in now and then.'

'Do they know you're a cop?' Dave wanted to know.

'Some know for sure. Others will have guessed it.'

'Is this going to mean trouble one day?'

'Nah, I don't think so. We all seem to be treating the place like a neutral zone. A couple of them have even bought me a drink.'

'Really? Have you heard anything useful from them?'

'Nothing I've acted on. There's been talk about a couple of break-ins at warehouses and the like, but nothing where anybody was hurt. I just keep my mouth shut.'

'Couldn't you get into trouble if someone found out?'

'Sure, but the real world doesn't exactly revolve the way some of the top brass think. Gotta live and let live. When I go to a friend's house, I leave being a cop behind. I drink in this place, so I'm not a cop when I'm here. Anywhere else I'm filth to the perps, but in here I'm just another guy having a wet one. And I treat them the same way. I run across them elsewhere doing something wrong and they're cooked. Tell you what; give me your home phone number. I might give you a call sometime and show you some of that real world I was talking about.'

~

Frank continued to drink in the pub and the friendship between he and Dave grew. The detective often came in around six in the evening and, when Dave was busy, chatted to the pub's most conservative client, known to staff as The General. Dave and the policeman attended a couple of Chelsea games, using tickets sent to the police station before every match.

~

One night, after a few drinks, Frank suggested they have some fun. He used his warrant card to forcefully gain entry to a private club for lesbians. They enjoyed a few free drinks and played a tense game of Scrabble with the owner and another woman, whilst the rest of the patrons looked on. Whenever the two women extracted money from the men, the onlookers cheered, whistled and applauded. Whenever the men took money from the women, an icy silence reigned. The atmosphere of hate in the small club was almost palpable. Whilst the game was progressing, two of the clientele heatedly kissed and cuddled in full view of everyone, daring either man to watch or make a remark. Frank and Dave won the scrabble game and left the club without paying for their drinks. Insults followed them out of the door.

~

On another day, Frank took Dave to a pub owned by an ex-policeman where the customers were almost exclusively cops and the women who chased them. The wall of the men's toilet carried the phone numbers of many women and gave a brief description of their attraction:

'Jane Gray 07911 999212 sucks until she draws blood.'

'Patricia Smith 07911 111191 wants a man to bring handcuffs and a truncheon along.'

'Barbara Denchfield 07911 001890 will do anything to marry a uniform.'

'Sharon Ponsomby 07911 554647 likes a 3some (1m2f).'

There were stabs at humour:

'Bollards to all traffic wardens.'

'My squeeze and my car hate sleeping policemen.'

Above the bar was a cage containing a colourful parrot that spoke with the same Yorkshire accent as its owner. The bird's favourite expression was, 'Oh oh, here come da judge.'

~

They had been drinking and watching a football game on television in another pub in Kensington, when a man at the bar suddenly announced in a loud voice, 'This country sucks!'

'Not while the football's on, pal,' someone advised him.

'That's all you care about? Football? Back home in Pakistan we don't waste our time watching football.'

'You're in England now, mate, so put a bleedin' lid on it.'

Dave noticed Frank put his drink down and give the man his attention.

'Allah would be most unhappy at this country's obsession with football.'

'Oh yeah? And what would Allah say if he knew you were drinking alcohol?'

Frank called out to the barman. 'Call an ambulance, quickly.'

'What the fuck for?'

'Cause this man needs one.' He took several quick steps toward the dark-skinned man, hit him in the solar plexus, kneed him in the groin and then smashed his knuckles into the man's temple as he doubled up. The policeman then snapped his knee up and into the man's face. Frank returned to the bar, picked up his glass, swallowed the scotch in one gulp, and motioned Dave to follow him out of the door. Once on the street, they walked at a fast pace for a couple of blocks before they found another pub.

'That was for Terry Waite. I hope I really hurt the bastard.'

'I thought Waite was held by the Lebanese.'

'What's the difference?'

'A lot. You kicked the shit out of that guy for the wrong reason.'

Frank paused and gave him a look. 'I was a bit surprised to see you didn't want a piece of it. Why don't we call it night, Dave? See you in a day or so.'

~

Three weeks later, the telephone rang at two o'clock on a Saturday morning. Dave had only been home half-an-hour and was still dressed.

'You like a new suit, Dave?'

'I wouldn't mind.'

'Pick you up outside your door in fifteen minutes.'

The car had three people in it. As Dave got into the back, he recognised two cops who had been in the pub on several occasions. During the journey, the policemen monitored Fire Brigade radio messages regarding a blaze at a warehouse. After about thirty minutes they arrived at an industrial estate, above which the sky was aglow. Bright sparks flew up in the draft created by the fire.

'The fire brigade responded to an alarm at this warehouse and tried to inform the owner. There was no response to a phone call and one of our lot was dispatched to the man's house and found the place empty. A neighbour reckoned the owner was on holiday in Bermuda, but she had no hotel name or means of contacting him. Said she had a key if we wanted it. Then we started a search for a possible insurer of the business-name that's apparently painted on a door at the back of the building but that revealed nothing. So, it's gonna take a while before we find some sort of representative and that, my friend, means it's our lucky day.'

There wasn't any great commotion caused by the fire. There were several fire-trucks and a lot of firemen present, but the scene was one of calm and professional people going about their business. Frank drove his car to the back of the building, away from the brightly-lit night sky and the few curious onlookers who had materialised.

A fireman had been about to stop them when he recognised the policemen. 'How's it hangin' fellers? This one's a doosie. There's others inside already. Make sure you save some for me.'

The four men got out of the car and entered the warehouse through a back door. Dave felt a little apprehensive about entering a burning building, but then reasoned that the roaring flames at the front were too far away to pose an immediate threat. Large cardboard cartons were strewn across the floor, their contents exposed. There were approximately twelve men inspecting or trying on clothing. Some wanted suits, others looked for sports-jackets and slacks. Frank, Dave and their two companions joined in the 'free-for-all'.

Frank nodded at a man who was about to leave with two suits, a green jacket, several shirts still in their plastic wrappers, and a handful of ties. 'It's been a while since we had one of these. My wardrobe was starting to look decidedly threadbare,' he said with a laugh.

One of the cops told Dave, 'Don't worry about sleeve or trouser length. Just find your waist size for strides and chest size for jackets. You can take everything to a tailor and have 'em altered to fit you.'

Dave was initially hesitant, but as he watched others steal the clothing he reasoned he was already an accessory to the crimes, so he might as well take advantage of the opportunity. Besides, what kind of situation might he be in if he took a high-minded stance? He appeased his conscience somewhat by limiting his haul to two suits, two cotton shirts, and two ties.

Frank was ahead of him as he left the warehouse and returned to the car. 'Keep your stuff on your knees. If we mix everything together in the boot, it'll take forever to sort out what belongs to whom.'

Men were exiting the burning warehouse weighed down with arms full of clothing. Dave counted fourteen cars neatly parked behind the warehouse. He assumed the firemen took the largest haul and they hadn't even started.

~

Dave's apprehension persisted. 'Won't it be obvious what happened here?'

'Nah,' one of the policemen responded. 'The firemen'll shepherd the fire to the pile of opened cartons and spilled clothing and make sure they're pretty much incinerated. The insurance company, if there is one, will accept the Fire Marshall's report and pay up. That's why scams like this are such a great deal for all concerned.'

'And I suppose when you guys come across something you call up your pals in the fire brigade?'

'You got it. Hi-jacked trucks containing booze or fags are great favourites. We always try to solve a crime a coupla days after it was committed. That way, we can say the clever bastards had time to dispose of all un-recovered merchandise. It can get a bit hairy sometimes, following these guys around before nicking them. There's been a couple that managed to lose us. Still, that's not too bad. The villains we do arrest get extra time for not revealing where they stashed the merchandise. They swear up hill and down dale that they're innocent but so, too, do the guilty ones. Besides, once they've been proven guilty of the original crime, who's gonna believe that they didn't get all the proceeds of it?'

'Then there's the robberies from jewellery shops, and the like,' Frank said with a laugh.

'I love ripping off the insurance companies,' one of the cops said as they drove back into the city. 'The shop owners do the same; inflating their losses. Makes it a little easier when I get the bills for my car and home insurance. When I read how much money the bastards make every year, something like this does me good. Puts the world right just a little bit.'

'Yeah. I'll tell you what though; it's time we got our hands on some booze again. My fuckin' wine cellar is almost empty.'

'You call that hole in the wall a wine cellar? You must be bleedin' jokin'.'

'No, no, you haven't seen what I've done to it. I took the wall out two feet into the driveway. I've got it rigged up real nice now. Trouble is the missus can't navigate the car down the driveway any more. She has to leave it out front all the time. Silly cow is scared stiff of scraping 'er car along the wall, or on the fence at the other side.'

Everyone laughed.

'You knocked the wall of your house out two feet just so as you could have a wine bar. What are you, nuts or something?'

'Not the whole wall; just the front room, up to the ceiling. I had a builder do it so as not to cause any structural damage.'

'You did all this so that you could store your wine in the house. Why do you think God invented garages, George?'

They reached Dave's building.

'Goodnight, mate.'

'See ya, pal.'

'By the way,' said Frank. 'Take the clothes you picked up tonight, plus what you're wearing now, to a dry cleaner Monday morning. Use one you've never used before. Once the shit's clean, you can take it to a tailor. Make sure he's new to you, too and make sure you pay everyone in cash.'

~

Frank appeared up at the pub the following week. Dave put a glass of Dewars and ice in front of him.

'Everything okay?' Frank asked.

'Fine. I see Chelsea won a game. How come they lose when we go to see them?'

'Swings and roundabouts, my friend.'

'Swings and roundabouts?'

'Yeah. You win some you lose some. Chelsea loses and you get a new wardrobe. They win and there's nothing on the horizon for us.'

'I would hate to think my luck was the reverse of Chelsea's. They might be a good team one day.'

'Don't worry about it. Something'll come along sooner or later. It always does.'

Dave served some other drinkers and then returned to where Frank was sitting.

'You know a solicitor?' Frank asked.

'No. Why? Do I need one?'

'Not that I know of. That'd be the day, wouldn't it? But if you ever do, you'll find it's not the best time to start looking for one.'

Frank tore half a page from his notebook and wrote a name and number on it. 'If you ever need one, call this guy. He's good and reasonably cheap. Ex-cop.'

And presumably someone who looks after cops and, coincidentally, their occasional fellow villains, Dave thought. He folded the paper and put in his back pocket. 'Thanks.'

Frank continued to drop into the pub for another couple of months. The two men went out drinking a few more times. They even got to see Chelsea win a game. Then, without explanation, the policeman never showed up again. Dave wondered if the man had run afoul of the top brass who had no idea of how the real world worked. Had Frank used the legal eagle whose number he had given Dave? Had that day materialised for him? Dave decided to hang on to the details of the solicitor. Maybe he should call him; put his foot in the door. Hopefully, he would never need him, but as Frank had said, it was better to be prepared.

Land Lover

The woman who Dave later knew as Cap'n Sam walked into the lounge bar just before lunch on a Tuesday in early January. She was a shorthaired brunette and, although her eye level was below Dave's, she was certainly taller than the majority of females that he checked out from his slatted wooden platform behind the bar. He figured she must be in her mid-to-late thirties. Her clothing had not come from a well-known designer's collection; scuffed black boots, blue jeans, a black V-necked sweater over a blue T-shirt and a navy pea coat. She wearily dropped her valise on the floor at the bar.

'You serve good food here?'

'It's not bad. It's not haute cuisine, but it's pretty good as far as pubs go. What're you after?'

'Something without beans, beef or broccoli. I've had those bees up to here.' She smiled as she brought her flat hand up to her throat. Her short-cut fingernails bore no polish. Her 'Geordie' intonation, whilst not too accentuated, did give her an aura of toughness.

'Well, we have Thai food and we have your sausage and eggs type food cooked by Thais. If I were you, I'd go for a nice curry of some sort.' Dave reached for a menu from a pile awaiting distribution to tables. 'Today's specials'll be on the board over there soon. What do you want to drink?'

'Rum and coke, please.'

'Coming right up.'

Dave put the tall, iced drink on the bar. 'Do you want to eat here at the bar, or on one of the tables?'

'The bar'll do fine, thanks.'

The Thai chef, known to the staff as Chee, entered the room with a red plastic milk crate and a packet of differently coloured chalks. He went to the wall where the blank blackboard with the word 'menu' at the top awaited attention, placed the crate on the floor and stepped up to perform his task. He took a list of the day's specials out of his pocket and started to copy them onto the board, using different coloured chalk for the various dishes. Green chalk for the green curry, red for red curry and white for rice were obvious choices. Other selections were not as easy to fathom.

'What do you recommend for today, Chee?' Dave called across the almost empty room.

The little man turned on his stand, almost losing his balance in the process. 'Led cully slimp in coconut sauce is best. Velly, velly good meal.' The man grinned, showing his recently acquired rows of white teeth.

'Thanks, Chee.' Dave turned to the woman, who was the only customer at the bar.

'There you have it. Straight from the horse's mouth, so to speak.'

'Fair enough. That's what I'll have. Thank you.'

'Got you a customer, Chee. One red curried shrimp in coconut sauce whenever you get to it.' Chee nodded his acknowledgement without pausing in his work. 'To be served at the bar,' Dave added as an afterthought.

The barman placed a second rum and coke in front of the woman who had taken off her jacket and spread it on the barstool next to where she sat.

'Thanks. Not many customers. Is it always this quiet?'

'No. You're here between sessions is all. When we first open, we have a flurry of customers for breakfast and then the unemployed regulars who come for the first drinks of the morning whilst they check the racing form for the day's meets.'

'Unemployed? How do they afford to drink and gamble if they are unemployed?'

'I've no idea. It's not as if the government pays that much to people on the dole. These guys somehow seem to be able to pay for several drinks on a daily basis. When they're done here, they cross the road to the bookies and place their bets. I think they then go home and watch the races on television.'

'Perhaps they know how to pick the winners.' The woman's facial expression indicated she didn't believe her words.

'Maybe. They usually leave around twelve-thirty or so, but they took off early today for some unknown reason. Perhaps there's a big race. Come five or ten past twelve, the lunch crowd'll start walking through the door. The salad and water crowd, we call 'em.' He put a red paper place-mat, a matching paper napkin, condiments and cutlery on the bar in front of the customer. 'My name's Dave. You?'

'Samantha. Samantha Banks. Pleased to meet you Dave.' She put out her hand and the barman shook it. 'Salad and water crowd?'

'Yeah. Mostly office workers. Mostly under thirty and mostly female. I guess the need to stay thin, combined with their low wages, dictates their diet. They're a pain in the neck, all rushing to the bar for their first glass of water at the same time. Thankfully, we get some construction workers in for their light, fluid lunches. If we have meat pie on the menu they'll eat that, but not much else.'

'In that case, why don't you make pies every day?'

'It's been tried, but Chee believes his status as chef precludes him from making such lowly food on a daily basis.'

'But the men still come here for their lunch every day?'

'I don't think they're *too* fussed about the meat pies. It's the young women they come for.'

'Aha! So, one way or another they come for the meat.'

Dave laughed. 'Not exactly. Most of the construction guys sit at the bar and leer at the girls. There's hardly any contact between the two groups.'

'Wishful thinking then.'

'Definitely wishful thinking for the guys. The girls don't want to know them.'

'What a pity; unrequited love.'

'More like unrequited lust.' Dave was tired of the topic of conversation. 'You live round here?'

'Close. I have a flat in Notting Hill. I've been away for a couple of weeks and feel too tired to make a meal for myself, so I thought I'd give the pub a chance to impress me.'

'Two weeks, huh? Where've you been?'

'I'm the captain of a ship that brings coal from the Northeast down to London.'

'Captain. Whoa. I'm impressed.'

'Don't be. It's a boring life.'

'Really! So why don't you move on?'

'I will eventually. Just have to gain enough experience before I can move on to the larger

ships. Pay my dues.'

'Well, I'm still impressed. It's not every day that I meet a ship's captain, let alone a female captain.'

'Careful, that was close to a sexist remark.'

'Sorry. It wasn't meant that way – I truly am impressed.'

'I was only joking. Considering I'm known as Cap'n Sam, I'm hardly in a position to complain about sexist labels.'

A young Thai girl appeared with the shrimp curry and so Dave left Samantha alone and went to help Ellen serve the customers that were now starting to arrive for their lunches – be they liquid or solid.

~

Most of the lunch crowd had departed by a-quarter-to-two and Dave again had a chance to talk to Samantha. 'You're still here.'

'Yes. Two hours for lunch is a rare luxury for me. It has been nice to relax, enjoy the good food and watch the goings-on of your other customers. You were right. The construction workers ogle the flesh but are rooted to their seats. If only they knew.'

'Perhaps they feel their hands and clothes are too dirty to start up a conversation with the cleanly dressed clerks.'

'I'm sure that's part of it, but there are also the educational and social barriers.'

'Well, I'm glad you enjoyed your meal. I would hate to think I'd recommended something you didn't like.'

'No, it was really good. Thank you. Oh, except for the ice-cream concoction I had. It was a bit of a let-down after the curry.'

'You should have asked. I would have steered you clear of the desserts. We don't make them here. We buy them from some food supply house and keep 'em in the freezer. I'll bet whatever you had was rock-hard when it was served.' Dave smiled.

'Yeah. That's how I ended up having two coffees. I'd drunk the first one way before the chocolate thingamabob was edible.'

'Do you want another drink?'

'No thanks. I'll settle up with you and go home for some much-needed sleep. Are you working tonight?'

'I get off at six.' Dave informed her as he gave her the bill.

'Want to take a lonely lady to dinner. My treat.'

Dave didn't hesitate, 'Sure. I'd love to.'

'How about I see you here at eight?'

'I'll be waiting.'

'Good. And there's no need for you to worry. I do own some dresses. You know what? Let me give you my number – just in case I sleep through the alarm. If I'm not here in time, call me.' The woman picked up the credit-card-receipt and wrote her number on its blank side. She handed the paper to Dave, together with a more than generous five-pound tip, and walked away.

~

In the weeks that followed, Dave saw Samantha every time she was able to get away from her coal carrying vessel, or collier as she called it. It wasn't often enough to prevent him from seeing other females and so the arrangement suited him well. He learned her other names were Audrey Nadine Dorothy and that she had been captain of her vessel, *Viking III*, for just over a year. The ship had a dead-weight of some ten-thousand-plus tons. Thirty-eight year-old Samantha's late father had been a seafarer with a sense of humour, hence her names. The *Viking III*'s cook lacked imagination and served only the most rudimentary food; baked beans, over-cooked beef and foul-smelling broccoli were his favourite basics. Almost all meals contained one or more of the 'bees'. The vessel's owners had promised Samantha a microwave oven and frozen dinners, but they had yet to arrive.

Each voyage took five to seven days, depending on weather and labour. It took up to forty-eight hours to sail north in ballast, depending on where they had to pick up their cargo. Loading could take up to a day and then a further two days to return to London. Another day to discharge the vessel and she was ready to set sail again. The vessel's owners usually had another charter lined up for immediate dispatch and so Samantha only got time off from her ship on an irregular basis. The owners employed at least two captains who rotated as stand-ins to relieve the tired and bored permanent masters.

Damp coal dust invariably coated the vessel after loading or discharging and so, as the *Viking III* headed north to pick up a fresh consignment, her crew cleaned her. Dave learned about Sam's life between eating and copulating. They rarely did anything else. Sam slept a lot when she was home because she spent most of her sea-time on the bridge. Whenever she had time to herself, she took care of what she missed most: food, sex and sleep.

~

By March, Dave was getting bored with the same routine. He reasoned it must be worse for Samantha. 'Can we do something other than fool around?'

She smiled. 'What did you have in mind?'

'Theatre, cinema, art galleries and such. We could go out with friends. Do you have any? You never mention them.'

'Not in London. I have some back home in Sunderland, but I rarely have enough time to visit them. I like the idea of going to see a film or a play, but I'm usually so tired I'm afraid I'd fall asleep. Tell you what. Why don't you do all the things you want to with your friends, while I stack up some zeds and then come round to see me at the end of the evening? I should think that'd be a great arrangement for a man. Only having to see a woman for sex after the night was over...and then only for two or three days every second week. Hell, if I owned a brewery as well, you would be in paradise.' Samantha's eyes sparkled as she grinned.

Dave grinned back, 'Sounds good, although it makes me feel a little selfish. What'll I do, call you an hour in advance to ask if you want some take-out food brought in? Give you a chance to take a shower and clean your teeth. What happens if you're wide-awake after the sex and I'm beat? You gonna be pissed?'

'Don't worry, we'll work it out. The arrangement is just as convenient for me as it is for you.'

'I suppose so, but I still feel as if I'm treating you unfairly.'

'Relax Dave. You'd just be doing what I want you to do.'

~

During Samantha's next shore leave, she put a new idea to Dave. 'How would you like to take a voyage with me? Come and see my little ship. Depending on how much time you can get off work, you could steam North with me and then either get a train back to London or stay on board for the return trip.'

'You sure? Do they allow civilians on cargo ships?'

'Of course they do. It's at the owner's and/or master's discretion, but it does happen. Mostly it's the master's wife and sometimes the kids. Some cargo lines even take paying passengers.'

'Sounds good. When can I go?'

~

A couple of weeks later, Dave arranged for a few days off work to accompany Captain Banks on board the good ship *Viking III*, which she was to take on the comparatively short voyage from Tilbury to Immingham.

'I'm afraid we're not in for the best of weather, Dave. According to the Met., it's going to blow and rain with a biblical force. You sure you're up to it, me handsome land lubber?' Her attempt at a sailor's brogue did not cover her 'Geordie' accent.

'If others can weather it, so can I.' His replied with more bravado than he felt. 'As long as your vessel is seaworthy, what do I have to worry about?'

'Well, we could get tossed around a bit. We only weigh just over ten thousand tons and that's not very big in a major storm. Plus, we're in ballast going up, which is the only part of the voyage you say you're able to sign up for.'

'We can't have everything. Don't worry about me, I'll be all right.'

'Fair enough. As I already told you, you'll be in my cabin. The steward will bring you your food. I'll be on the bridge most of the time but I'll join you for some recreation whenever the situation allows. You'll be able to spend time with me on the bridge, as well. I guess our roles are going to be somewhat reversed for the next forty-eight hours.'

~

As they walked up the rickety and noisy aluminium steps suspended over the side of the vessel, Dave took hold of the rail to steady himself. The slack chain felt cold and gritty and he lifted his hand to find his palm and fingers coated with wet coal dust. There was nothing on which to wipe his hand clean, so he put it back on the rail and continued to the top. When they reached the deck, Samantha introduced him to her first mate.

'Dave, this is Bob Donnelly. Bob, Dave Wilson. He's going to Immingham with us.'

'Aye, aye Cap'n. Pleased ta meecha Mr. Wilson. Ya might be needin' this, I fancy.' He proffered a dirty towel.

Dave took the towel and wiped his palm clean before shaking hands with the seaman.

'Thanks.'

~

In the cabin, Dave unpacked his grip and stowed his clothes in a drawer Samantha had assigned him. There was a gentle swell on the Thames but it was no greater than he'd expected. When Sam left to do her job, he inspected the area. It was small for one person, never mind two. When he looked out of the porthole, he saw green fields and dark clouds.

At first, Dave didn't notice the increase in the vessel's motion. As there was nothing to watch on afternoon television, he lay on the bunk and read a book.

As daylight began to fade there was a knock on the door. 'Come in,' he said.

The door opened slowly at first, but then the movement of the ship caused it to crash into the end of the bunk with a loud bang. 'Sorry, suh. It's getting' a bit rough an' I didna want to spill yer meal,' said a small, dishevelled man with unkempt hair, a dirty tee-shirt and jeans. He balanced a tray with one hand and was mindful of the swinging cabin door with the other as he stepped into the cabin.

'Will ya take yer pew here at the desk, please suh,' was not a question.

'Ah canna put the soup doon, or it'll be all over the place. If you could tack the bowl, ah'll secure the plate as best ah can on the desk.'

Dave suddenly realised how much the ship was rolling. The noise made by the storm made hearing the man's words difficult.

'Sit at the corner o' the desk and wrap yer pins around the leg,' he souted. 'When ah give ya the soup, you'll 'ave ta 'old it in one hand an' move yer arm back an' forth in the opposite direction to the vessel's movement. Like so, suh.' The man took the soup bowl from the tray and demonstrated the required action. It was a comical situation with both the soup bowl and the tray swinging from side to side whilst the man, with knees bent, maintained his balance. Dave watched, his eyes swivelling from left to right and right to left like a spectator at a tennis match. The landlubber reached with both hands for the soup, took it and settled the bowl in his upturned left hand. The steward then took off the lid. Dave started the swinging movement but was concerned at the heat of the bowl. The steward put the covered plate on the desk top, using books and instruments to wedge it in place against the miniature brass railing that ran along the desk's perimeter. The heat from the soup bowl was becoming uncomfortable.

'Go ahead, suh. Use yer right 'and to spoon some o' the liquid into yer mout. You'll soon get the hang of it,' the steward shouted, revealing two pink gums and three yellow teeth.

Dave scooped up a half-spoon of the greenish liquid and drank it, all the while swinging the hot bowl from side to side. The stuff tasted terrible. He smiled. 'Very good. Thank you. I think I'll be okay now. I'm sure you have other mouths to feed, so I don't want to keep you.'

The steward nodded his head, mouthed 'Bon appetite, suh,' and left.

Dave rested the soup spoon on the side of the soup bowl and changed hands. He breathed cool air onto his hot palm. The right hand continued the motion without a hitch, but the spoon slid into the bowl and drowned in the viscous liquid. He had no intention of eating the soup that he assumed was cream of broccoli (not that the taste gave any clue), but he couldn't leave it to be subject to the ship's violent motions. He fished around the still hot mixture and rescued the spoon, then got gingerly to his feet and zigzagged his way across the cabin to the bathroom, or 'head' as Samantha had called it. He staggered to his left and right. He was propelled forwards and then backwards, all the time balancing the bowl like a drunken waiter. Twice he almost lost the entire contents, but recovered his balance in time to limit the spillage to a couple of thick splotches. He emptied the green/grey liquid into the toilet, rinsed the spoon and bowl in a tiny aluminium washbasin and then realised that the clean utensils would alert the steward to what he had done.

He staggered back across the cabin to the desk and wondered what to do with the soup bowl. He pulled his shirt flaps out of his trousers and wiped the bowl dry. Not wanting the bowl to become a flying missile, he made his wavy way to the bed and secured the object under the tightly stretched blanket. He put the spoon in his pants pocket. Dave then took the napkin, which he belatedly realised could have been used to dry the bowl and spoon, dropped to his knees and cleaned the spilled soup from the black metal floor. Once he had mopped up, he tried to get to his feet. The ship's pitching made it difficult for him to regain an upright position and he banged his temple against the side of the wooden bunk before a dramatic dip caused him to roll across the cabin.

When he had re-installed himself at the desk with his legs wrapped tightly around one of its supports, Dave unclipped the lid from the plate holding the main course. The sight of the grey looking beef with grey boiled potatoes, limp greenery and thick, lumpy gravy took away what remained of his appetite. He quickly re-clipped the cover and re-wedged the plate on the desk's surface. He used the soiled napkin to cushion the edge of the pot plate against the brass railing.

The pitching of the vessel was starting to alarm Dave. He remembered his cavalier disregard of Sam's warning about the weather and promised himself not to complain about the conditions. Reading proved to be too much of a challenge, so he switched on the television in an attempt to take his mind off the situation. An American police drama had just started and he lay down on the bunk to watch it. The soup bowl made an uncomfortable bulge. Dave flipped onto his stomach, leaned over the edge of the bunk and pulled open a drawer beneath the mattress. He re-arranged the contents to make room for the soup bowl.

The noise of the storm was a constant roar and he was unable to hear any sound from the television. Thirty-five minutes later, the picture faded to chaotic static. He didn't have the will to raise himself from his safe position, so he lay and watched a quiz game materialise on the screen. A particularly violent roll almost dislodged him from the bunk, but he saved himself by clutching onto the wooden safety railing that ran along the outer side of the bed. A drawer suddenly flew out of the chest and landed on the floor with a loud clatter. Dave carefully got up and endeavoured to repack the items whilst holding onto the edge of the bunk. He was trying to figure out how he could put the drawer back in its place when the telephone, which sat in a special cradle on the desk, rang. He waited for the ship to roll in the right direction, and then made a lunge for the desk.

'Dave. Samantha. How are you managing in this horrible storm?' Sam was screaming into the phone to overcome the noise of the weather. 'You must be getting thrown all over the place, you poor man. I'll be down to see you as soon as I can, but I'm afraid it won't be for a while. If you look on the deckhead you'll see…'

'What's a deckhead?' Dave shouted above the din.

'Ceiling to you. Sorry. If you look on the ceiling you'll see three strips of metal bolted there.'

A sudden lurch threw Dave across the cabin. He stretched out his arm for protection but still banged his rib-cage against the side of the bunk. The strong telephone cable snapped taut and when Dave was propelled in a different direction, the receiver jerked out of his hand. He pulled his way back and picked it up. 'Okay, I see them.'

'Good.' There was humour in her voice. 'Now, I want you to insert them into the slots on the chest of drawers, the drawers under the bunk and the desk. Will you do that for me?'

'Sure.'

'Thank you, darling. See you in a while.'

He had to put the drawer back into the chest first. He was unable to keep his balance and line up the runners until luck took charge. A pitch made him fall against the chest and the drawer miraculously slid into position. He banged a couple of his fingers but the drawer stayed in place.

It took quite a while to unbolt the slats. Dave found he needed both hands to free the metal strips and both hands to maintain his balance. He worked feverishly, worried that drawers might fly out of the chest again. One of the bars fell on his head and caused a lump to grow. He crashed into the walls and the bunk many times. He knew he was bruised in several areas and found he was trying to protect a couple of badly bashed sites. Once the bars were free, he laid two of them under the blanket on the bunk before forcing his way to the chest of drawers. He could see where to insert the restrainer, but positioning the object presented a challenge. After several attempts, during which time he staggered backwards and forwards, he managed to slide the bar down the runners. Each time he came to the top of one of the four drawers, he had to slam it shut and speedily advance the slat over the level surface. Once the bar reached the floor it snapped into place. He repeated the manoeuvre at the desk and below the bunk.

He took off his shoes but nothing more, before getting under the woollen blanket on the bunk. Once covered, he purposefully tucked the edges of the top bedding under the mattress to secure himself in place. The television program had changed to an action movie that Dave was able to follow without needing to hear dialogue. He felt reasonably safe under the blanket but he knew he would not sleep until he was thoroughly exhausted.

~

Samantha appeared sometime later. The ship was still pitching and rolling, but the captain seemed more able to maintain her balance than Dave. 'Having fun?'

'They should include something like this at those theme parks Disney builds.'

'It's a thought. Maybe I'll write to them.' The woman smiled down at Dave who was still prone on the bunk. 'Bob Donnelly is on the bridge now so I can have a little time to myself. Did you enjoy your meal?'

'I hardly touched it. The soup went down the toilet and the main course is still on your desk, trapped between that little fence and your books and stuff.' He waved an arm in the general direction of the table.

'That little fence is called a fiddle,' Samantha said as she removed her clothes. 'What a waste. Good food like that.' Her eyes smiled as she bent to remove her boots. 'Do you have the restraining straps on?'

'What restraining straps?'

Sam snapped the bar free of its mooring and opened the drawer beneath the bed. 'What's the soup dish doing in here?' she asked with a laugh.

'I didn't want to get off the bunk and couldn't think of anywhere else to put it,' Dave sheepishly replied.

'Well, this'll do I suppose,' the near naked Sam laughingly approved.

~

'Why do the television programs fade away?' Dave wanted to know.

'We lose the signal as we progress up the coast. The trick is to try and watch a program that doesn't last for more than an hour.'

'Makes things a bit inconvenient'

'That's life on the ocean waves for you. All right. Here's the drill. You're going to lie there and I'm going to tie a couple of straps up here for me to hang onto.' Samantha started to knot a yellow nylon strap around one of the hooks that ran the length of the wall ('bulkhead', she called it). 'When I climb on top of you, the motion of the ship should make for an interesting fuck. It's going to be a mind game, not being able to touch each other properly. We'll use our eyes. It'll be like tantric sex, except you'll be inside me. I know that doesn't make sense, but you'll see what I mean. What do you think?'

'Let's go, Cap'n!'

'That's what I hoped you'd say.'

Dave meant to rip off his covering blanket with a show of passion, but he had tucked it in place so securely that it took three attempts before he was unwrapped. Naked Samantha settled on top of him, holding on to the yellow strap with one hand while helping him strip off his clothes with the other.

~

The ship's captain had returned to duty on the bridge after securing Dave in the bunk. He slept through the night to the next day, which was sunny and calm. When he awoke he examined his painful body and felt his bruises before getting dressed.

He had just fixed the last restrainer in place on the deckhead when the steward arrived. 'An' the top o' da mornin' to yuh, suh.'

'Morning. Quite a night.'

'Oh yes, but today is fine and dandy, suh.' He laid a plate of bacon, eggs, baked beans and toast on the desktop. There was hot tea in a spill-proof container. 'Do ya have the dishes from last night's meal, suh?'

'Oh. Yeah.' He nodded at the desk. 'Well, there's the plate. I'm afraid, what with the weather and all, I didn't eat any of it. My stomach isn't used to such treatment. I'll just get the soup bowl.' Dave felt mortified as he pulled open the drawer beneath the bunk and retrieved the dish.

'Ah yes, suh, a very safe place for it that was.'

Dave looked at the man's face, but there wasn't a hint of ridicule or sarcasm on it. The steward maintained the blank look as the passenger took the soup spoon out of his pocket. Dave felt as he had one day in school when the geography teacher had demanded he surrender a 'Playboy' magazine he had been reading under his desk during class.

~

Samantha called and asked him up to the bridge after breakfast. 'Turn left out of the cabin, up a flight of eight steps and you'll be with me.'

Dave swallowed the last of the tea and went up to join her.

Sam gave him a 'good morning' peck on his cheek, 'We lost a little time last night, but we should arrive at Immingham by early evening. You can take a taxi to the station and catch a train back to 'the smoke'. That all right with you?'

'Fine. Thank you. Hell of a view from up here.'

'Yes it is. I need to be able to see what is going on all around me.'

Dave walked to one side of the bridge and looked down into the water. He walked to the other side to do the same. In front of the bridge he saw the covered holds where the coal would be loaded. 'The ship looks pretty clean to me.'

'It is. The storm cleaned her up nicely. It's a mixed blessing for the crew. They get a violent trip but they don't have to clean the outside of the ship. In fairness though, their voyage wasn't as violent as yours was last night. Their quarters are closer to the keel and the roll down there is less severe than it is up here.'

'I should have joined them.' Dave smiled.

'You could have – but then you'd have missed out on the action.'

'Good point.'

~

Viking III docked at Immingham at low tide. The ship rested alongside a stone wall that looked to rise at least twenty feet above the vessel's deck and Dave wondered how one went ashore. A ladder with metal wheels on the end, leaned from the ship's deck against the side of the dock. As the ship rose and fell on the slight swell, the ladder moved up and down the wall. Samantha did not want any member of the crew to witness a parting kiss, so she and Dave bade their farewells on the otherwise empty ship's bridge.

'Couldn't we have docked at high tide?' Dave asked his lover.

'Let the steward take your bag up the ladder. He's done it many times before.'

'I think I have to do it myself.'

'For God's sake, why?'

'I lost a lot of face retrieving the soup bowl from the drawer under the bunk this morning, and fishing the soupspoon from my pocket didn't help. Maybe I can get my dignity back by getting myself and my belongings up that ladder.'

Samantha nodded. 'Okay, if you really insist.'

'I do.'

'Well, watch it from here for a while so you can get your timing right. It all depends on how fast you plan to go up the ladder.'

'Normal speed.'

'That's normal speed for a land lubber, I take it.'

'I suppose so. Why?'

'I estimate it'll take you one-and-a-half swells to get up the ladder, so you'll need to start climbing when the top is halfway through the 'down' motion. Watch it and see.'

Dave studied the movement of the ladder for a few minutes. 'Okay, I think I've got it.'

'One tip. You'll be better off if you can just walk up the ladder without using your hands. You'll have your overnight bag in one hand and the other will be free if you need it, but you'll probably find it easier if you walk up the rungs in an upright position.'

'Jesus Christ, Sam! What's next, Blackpool Tower Circus?'

'You'll do fine.' She smiled and gave him a kiss. 'See you in London.'

~

The movement of the ladder against the wall looked greater when Dave viewed it from the deck. The wheels made a squeaking noise as they rubbed against the wall. Dave noticed one of them had rusted into immobility and the occasional spark flew as it grated against the wall's grey stone. The steward stood on the deck, his face creased in a toothy grin. Dave watched the ladder rise and fall. He noticed it was covered with wet coal dust and surmised the crew kept it in one of the holds. Other crewmembers appeared, not wanting to miss the anticipated humiliation of the landlubber that slept with their captain.

The collier dipped and the ladder began its downward motion. Dave stepped onto the bottom rung and started his ascent. As Sam had suggested, it was easier than he had imagined. Elation surged in him as he stepped from rung to rung and was soon near the top of the wooden ladder. He stopped, his feet on the fourth and fifth rungs from the top. He noticed his left toecap was only two or three inches away from the wall. The ladder began to rise again. He held onto his bag with his right hand and let the fingers of his left hand lightly feel their way up the wall as he rose in its face. He knew the ladder would not reach the top of the wall but as it rose he slowly climbed the last few rungs. When he put his foot on the penultimate rung, his toe touched the wall and almost caused him to lose his balance. He quickly stepped up and onto the quay. Relief flooded through him. He had made it on his own and without making a fool of himself. The crew applauded and he turned to look down at the deck. The steward smiled up at him and gave a half-hearted salute. He raised his eyes and found himself almost level with Samantha who was standing on the edge of the bridge with a big smile on her face.

'So glad you didn't fall in.'

'Me, too.' He smiled back at her

Dave never dated Samantha again. She had been into the pub and graciously accepted that Dave had moved on. He reasoned it was probably the story of her life and felt a little sorry for her. She still made regular visits to the Coach House and told Dave about her latest voyage before picking up one of the construction workers to take home with her. He crumpled the credit card receipt and threw it into the rubbish bin.

Hot Tip

Dave had no trouble recalling Graham Derby. The man was a stockbroker Dave had overheard discussing a promising new stock. Derby had urged another man to invest as much as he could afford in the initial public offering and to sell the stock by lunchtime on the day of issue. Dave had borrowed money from everyone he could, including a loan-shark, and taken it to a different stockbroker to invest for him. He had almost made himself sick with worry that the conversation was drink inspired or that Derby was a fool. He bought seven-thousand, eight-hundred-and-forty shares at one pound, twenty-five each and sold them at one p.m. on the same day for seven pounds, thirty-five, realising a profit of forty-seven thousand, eight-hundred and twenty-four pounds, less commission. After he had repaid everybody and settled every outstanding debt, he still had a tidy sum of money. It was enough to allow him to continue working at the job he so enjoyed. Derby had somehow known about Dave's windfall and cautioned him regarding insider trading and the wisdom of keeping one's mouth firmly shut. Although Derby openly told him about other trades, Dave never again made such a killing. The one risk had been enough for Dave and he now kept the money invested in blue-chip stock.

Dave made a note of the man's details in the new diary and filed the business card in the back pouch.

In Case of Emergency

Katherine Madison had walked into the pub and asked for a pint of Pepsi with lots of ice. The woman hadn't looked well but as she hadn't ordered alcohol, Dave decided to serve her. 'Why don't you take a seat by the window and I'll bring the drink over to you.' The barman packed the glass with ice, then used the soda gun to squirt Pepsi into it. As he waited for the liquid to settle, he watched the sickly woman wend her way towards a table. She progressed slowly, weaving a little as she went. She kept her extended right hand at waist height, as if ready to reach for support. Dave put a straw into the glass and went to where the woman stood. He put the refreshment down and gently put his hand under the woman's elbow to support her while she eased herself into a chair. He felt her tremble and noticed the sheen of perspiration on her face.

'Are you okay?' he inquired.

'I will be,' she replied. 'Just give me a couple of minutes.'

He returned to the bar and pulled two pints of best bitter for a couple of men who had been waiting patiently.

'She doesn't look too hot,' one of them observed.

'Yeah, well, I'm off in ten minutes, so she'll be someone else's problem,' Dave said.

~

Ellen, Dave's replacement, walked into the pub at ten-to-seven. She sat on the civilian side of the bar and asked for a glass of water. 'How's it going?'

'Same old shit, 'cept for the woman at the table over there. She's pretty shaky. Got the sweats an' tremors and looks like hell.'

'Just done the deed with you, huh?' Ellen asked with a grin.

'You have to be joking!' Dave pretended to shudder at the thought, and then put on a serious face. 'Who knows? Maybe she's got the flu, or something.'

Ellen found his easy acceptance of the situation irksome. 'Hey, if she's strung out on someting we have to get her ouda here. You know Marty. She's so paranoid about drugs, she'd fire both of us.'

'Well, my lovely Irish friend, you can do what you want. It's now seven o'clock, so I'm off and you're on.' Dave turned away from the bar.

'You're such a sweetheart, Dave.'

'Aren't I though,' he said with a laugh.

~

He went to the staff room to take off his black bow tie and waistcoat and hang them in his locker. He also added drinks customers had bought him and which he hadn't drunk to a tally he kept. The addition brought the total measures of scotch owed to sixteen. He made a mental note to ask Marty to give him a bottle. As he re-entered the bar, he saw the sickly customer place her hands on the table and push down as she tried to rise from her chair. She looked unsteady, so Dave strode across the room, arriving in time to catch her as she collapsed. He lowered her to the floor and wondered if he was supposed to check if any of her clothing was too tight. To hell with it. He wasn't about to start feeling up a woman in full view of so many curious customers.

'Ellen, call an ambulance,' he shouted.

'Already ahead of you.'

Dave rolled the jacket he had been about to don into a ball and slipped it under the comatose woman's head. He instructed one of the customers to pass him the woman's handbag, which he placed beside her inert body.

'Okay folks. Let's give the lady some air.'

He got up and gently pushed a couple of people back. The rest took their cue and retreated two or three steps.

~

An ambulance arrived a few minutes later.

'What happened?' one of the paramedics asked.

'No idea, mate. She came in, ordered a Pepsi and sat at a table,' Dave explained. 'She looked a bit under the weather and then she collapsed when she tried to get up from her chair.'

The second paramedic looked at the circle of inquisitive customers. 'Anybody know who she is?'

'I don't think so,' Dave answered. 'I'm a barman here and I've never seen her before. Do you know her, Ellen?'

'Never seen her before today,' the barmaid called back.

'Let's have a look in her handbag then.' The man stretched for the shiny black faux-leather bag.

'Miss Katherine Madison,' the medical man murmured. 'Heyup, she's supposed to go for dialysis three times a week. Why's that, lady? You an alchy that's done your liver in?'

The two paramedics checked her breathing and her vital signs, inserted a drip into her arm, and then lifted the still motionless patient onto a stretcher.

'Do you need me anymore?' Dave asked.

'You'd better come along so you can tell the doctors what happened.'

'What? There's not much to tell really,' said Dave, half-heartedly trying to excuse himself from the journey.

'You should go along wid her, Dave. Make sure duh pub's interests're covered,' Ellen called out to him. 'I'll tell Marty what yer doing and tell 'er she owes ya duh time.'

The medic gave a sympathetic grin. 'You never know. It might be important.'

At the hospital, the paramedics placed Miss Madison on a gurney and wheeled it to the emergency room where they gave a brief description of what they had found and done. One of them introduced Dave as a witness to the woman's collapse. They completed the paperwork, replenished their medical supplies and left. A man in a pale-green smock wheeled the gurney into an area containing cubicles partitioned by short, flimsy curtains that matched his uniform. Without a word he abandoned a slightly self-conscious Dave with his newfound acquaintance.

The cubicle was an open square. Dave looked out, surveyed the part of the emergency room visible to him, and saw an unused chair against a far wall. He collected it, draped his jacket over it and was about to sit when a blonde-haired nurse breezed into the area, making the curtains swirl in her wake. She checked the patient's details recorded on a clipboard, then looked at Dave.

'Hi. I know how she is, what about you?' She didn't wait for an answer. 'The doctor should be here soon. Is there anything you need in the meantime?'

The lovely woman's cheerful attitude brought a smile to Dave's face. 'No, I'm all right, thanks. I don't know about this woman, though. She's been unconscious for a long time.'

'That's probably her defence mechanism taking care of her. Don't worry about it. I'll be around for the rest of the night, so let me know if you need anything.'

The nurse left in the same business-like manner with which she had arrived, leaving a trace of the scent of her shampoo in the air. Dave had been about to ask if his presence was really needed, but the chance of getting a date with the lovely nurse convinced him he was a vital part of Miss Madison's diagnostic process.

He settled himself for a long wait. He recalled the nurse had said only that the doctor *should* appear soon. Dave started to take inventory of the uniformed woman. She was about five-feet-six with a trim figure and smiling blue eyes. Around her neck she wore a simple gold cross on a thin chain. He hadn't seen much of her legs, but the departing calves and ankles had seemed shapely enough, despite her flatties. He regretted not getting her name. As a nurse, she surely must have worn a badge or some kind of identification. How could he have missed it? If she didn't re-appear soon, he would have to think up some excuse to go looking for her. A trip to the bathroom would do it.

He sensed activity behind the curtain on the far side of

Katherine and listened to a conversation he assumed was about a patient.

'Drunk out of his mind. Stupid bastard got himself thrown out of a pub for being obnoxious and decided to return with a cricket bat. He trashed the windshields of a few cars in the vicinity and then the pub's windows before going back into the bar to take his revenge. Unfortunately for him, some guys took away his bat and used it to beat the shit out of him. When we got there, we saved him from further punishment and he tries to attack *us*. Grateful bastard poked a finger in my partner's eye. I think I'll just keep him company until we decide whether or not we're going to add the charge of assaulting a police officer.'

Dave assessed the black-stocking legs visible below the partitioning curtain, but couldn't tell whether they belonged to the same blonde nurse or not. The muffled sound of a small explosion broke the momentary silence.

'Jesus Aitch Christ!' the policeman cursed in a shouted whisper. 'If this guy is going to fart all night, I'm gonna get really pissed at him. You got anything to put a stop to it?'

'Not for a comatose patient, we don't.' The laughing voice didn't sound like his nurse.

The putrid apple smell of the drunken man's gas reached Dave.

'Surely there must be something?' The man with the dark blue serge trousers pleaded.

The nurse left with a 'Sorry' in her wake.

The policeman acknowledged Dave's unseen presence. 'Enough to put you off scrumpy for the rest of your life, ain't it? You wonder why wives put up with it night after night.'

The sound of a woman's screams grew closer as she neared the emergency room. 'Hang on, luv,' a female voice pleaded. 'We'll have something for your pain in a sec.'

'My daughter; where's my daughter?' the woman screamed out.

'She's fine, Abby…it is Abby isn't it?' a man asked her. 'Your daughter's receiving treatment for a broken leg but other than that, she's all right.'

The woman sobbed, then shrieked again. Once she regained control, she pleaded, 'You wouldn't lie to me would you? I need to know the truth about her. Hiding the truth from me won't make me feel any better.'

'I swear it's the truth, Abby; your daughter's fine.'

Somewhere else in the area, a team of medical people fought to save, what Dave later learned, was a botched suicide attempt. 'I've got a pulse,' a man shouted. The room seemed to breathe a sigh of relief.

Another chair appeared a few feet from the area where Dave and his still comatose charge waited. A different nurse led a middle-aged lady by the arm and sat her on the chair where she had a direct line of sight into the curtained cubical occupied by Dave and Miss Madison. 'You'll have to wait here until the doctor can see you, Miss Needham. If a cubicle becomes free, I'll come and get you.'

~

A loud beeping noise suddenly erupted and medical staff rushed to answer its call. 'She's crashed again!'

Abby screamed.

The woman in the chair made a quick dash to where Dave sat, reached under the gurney on which Miss Madison lay, grabbed the waste bin and vomited into it.

The man in the next space gave off a long, loud fart.

'I can't get a pulse. She's in VF. Get the defib!' After a short pause the same voice shouted again, 'Stand back. Clear!'

The defibrillators made the body thump, which added to the bedlam. The vomiting woman retreated to the passageway, taking the bin with her. Abby moaned. Puddles of orangey vomit had missed the bin and splattered the floor. Two unidentified orange lumps decorated the toecap of Dave's right shoe. The defibrillators thumped again. The woman heaved again and the man let out another fart. Dave could feel his own stomach churn and he concentrated on maintaining his self-control. He unsuccessfully sought out the smell of anything medical, but in the end he had to bury his face in his unwashed hands and inhale the now stale odours of cigarettes and beer.

~

A doctor arrived, unhappily sniffing the air as he entered the curtained cubicle. Dave's nurse followed and he remembered to check her identity badge. 'Noreena Phillips, RN'.

'Anyone found out if she's missed dialysis?' the medical man asked.

'She missed yesterday's appointment and apparently has a spotty attendance record,' Noreena advised him.

'Who are you?' the doctor wanted to know of Dave.

'He witnessed the woman's collapse,' Noreena answered for him as she extracted three tissues from a slot in the surface of a trolley that had arrived with the doctor. She handed them to Dave. 'For your shoe,' she said with a smile.

'How did she seem at the time?' asked the man identified as Dr. Mohammed Aziz.

Dave was bending over his shoe but he swivelled his head and looked up at the doctor. 'Pale, perspiring, and unsteady on her feet. She wanted a Pepsi-Cola with lots of ice.'

'Hmmm. Will you make the necessary arrangements, nurse?'

'Yes, doctor.'

Dr. Aziz silently made some notes, and the man in the next cubicle farted again.

'Jesus fuck!' the policeman whispered behind the curtain.

'What happens now?' Dave inquired of the beautiful nurse. He looked for somewhere to deposit the soiled tissues.

Noreena took them from his hand. 'We'll see if anyone is available at the dialysis centre. If there is, we'll send Katherine over there in an ambulance.'

'I guess I should stay with her 'til then?' said a hopeful Dave. His lust for the lovely nurse was greater than his desire to get out of the stinking environment. He wanted to arrange a date with Noreena, even though the situation made the quest seem almost irreverent. If he stayed long enough, perhaps a more suitable moment might present itself.

'That's very thoughtful of you,' Noreena said with a knowing smile.

The drunk in the next cubicle farted yet again and the cop left the area for some respite. 'I'll be back in a minute,' he informed anyone who was listening.

The lady on the chair was now dry-heaving over the can.

A cold voice declared the suicide a success.

Abby's screams had subsided to low moans.

~

Half an hour later, Dave decided to find Noreena and ask for directions to the bathroom. Trying to appear lost, he homed on her voice and almost bumped into her as he turned the first corner out of the emergency room. She was leaning against the wall, chatting with two other nurses and sipping a steaming drink.

'Follow the red stripe on the floor, keeping your eyes on the right-hand doors as you go. You'll soon find it.' Noreena grinned at him.

'Thanks. How did you know?'

'What else would you be doing if you weren't stalking me?' Her eyes twinkled with mischief.

~

On his return, Dave found a well-dressed, blue haired woman loudly complaining that she wasn't receiving the treatment she felt she needed. She didn't seem injured or sick to Dave. He went to the cubicle where the now conscious Katherine still lay. She seemed even paler.

'Who are you?' she wanted to know.

'Hi. I work at the pub. You came in for a drink of Pepsi. Don't you remember?'

'Vaguely,' she whispered.

Dave told her of all that had transpired since she had tried to get up from the table in the pub. The man beyond the curtain farted loudly again. Katherine seemed too out of kilter to notice. Dave looked around for the chair, but it had disappeared, together with his jacket. He left Katherine and went to look for his expensive leather garment. At the far end of the nurses' desk sat the loud lady with the lacquered blue hairdo. As Dave approached, he could see his jacket on the back of the chair.

'Would you jump into my grave as quickly?' he asked angrily.

'I *beg* your pardon?' replied the haughty woman.

'Did you take that chair from the cubicle at the end of the room?'

'I most certainly did. It wasn't being used and I was in need of it.'

'And my jacket, too?'

'Take your jacket. Please. It smells of cigarettes. I don't know how anyone could wear such a thing.'

Dave snatched the jacket and dragged it across the woman's elaborate hair. He was a little peeved to notice that not a single strand was disturbed.

~

A smiling Noreena appeared at the cubicle with another chair.

'Here you are, Sir Galahad.'

He took it from her hand. 'Thank you. Listen; are you married, or dating somebody, or anything?'

'Or anything? What's that supposed to mean?' Dave opened his mouth to explain but the nurse continued. 'No, I'm not doing anything with anyone right now, but what business is that of yours?'

'Well, none I suppose, but I'd like to see you outside of this place and thought I'd better establish whether or not you're 'off the market'.'

Noreena smiled. 'And what kind of market would that be?'

The conversation wasn't going the way Dave had planned. 'Sorry. I used that expression instead of asking if you were available, which I know from experience can get me into trouble. I guess I just jumped out of the frying pan and into the fire.' He took a breath and started again, 'Would you, Nurse Phillips, be offended if I were to ask you out on a date?'

'Here,' she said as she thrust a piece of white plastic-like paper into his shirt pocket. 'Given the limitation of your sensitive vocabulary, it's going to be really interesting if the subject of sex comes up. Now you'll have to go. The ambulance is here and Katherine is leaving us.'

Dave wandered over to the nurses' desk and pulled the paper out of his pocket. It was part of a wrapping for a bandage and on it was written Noreena's name and telephone number. As he walked out of the building he breathed in the clean night air. It had never smelled so sweet.

He had dated Noreena for about four months. In the end, the demand made by their jobs so limited their time together, the relationship had died a slow death. He had liked Noreena but he was with Jane now so there was point in keeping the nurse's number. He crushed the wrapper in his hand and dropped it in into the bin where it promptly unfolded itself.

Bonnie Scotland

Dave stared at a number on a pink tissue and, for a moment, couldn't recall who had given it to him. Then the memory suddenly surfaced. Scotland! He'd never been to Scotland, so when he had three consecutive days off in July, he'd gone to Glasgow.

The train had raced through small stations but behind the deserted platforms, Dave had seen glimpses of small houses in which, he assumed, lived stationmasters and their families. The country day had been windy, causing washing on clotheslines in the small gardens to flap at a high angle. Colourful patches of well-maintained lawns and flowerbeds evidenced managing a small station left plenty of time for weeding, pruning, mowing, and whatever else one does in a garden.

At Lancaster, where Dave could see purple mountains in the distance, a new passenger got his attention. The woman was in her late twenties with black hair and hazel eyes. Her nicely tanned shoulders made a pleasing contrast to her yellow halter. The garment must have been all of four inches wide and held in place by breasts that bulged above the piece and proclaimed their existence proudly. In her bellybutton was a shiny silver stud. Her accompanying children were a slight drawback.

The youngest daughter was very attentive. 'Can I get you a drink, mummy?' she asked as she leaned over from the seat behind her mother. 'Do you want a sandwich, mummy?'

Many of the men in the carriage suddenly found they had to go to the buffet car, visit the bathroom, or stretch their legs. A young woman of about eighteen, who sported a white-blonde crew cut, wore silver jewellery and black leather clothing, also took an interest. Her leather pants squeaked on her seat as she twisted round to get a better look.

~

As the train arrived at the next station, Oxenholme The Lake District, a woman passed Dave with a suitcase in her right hand and a hefty looking handbag wedged under her right arm. She held a mobile phone to her ear with her left hand.

'Will you hurry up for God's sake; I'm trying to get off the train.' There was a short silence before she exploded with exasperation. 'But I don't want to be found. Why'd you tell him I was travelling here? You haven't done me a favour at all.'

Dave expected her to retake her seat, but then saw her on the platform apparently shouting at her caller.

He found the name of the town amusing. He imagined inhabitants declaring to the inquisitive, 'Hi. I'm from Oxenholme The Lake District'

Another mother came on board with her nine or ten-year old son dressed in a light grey suit with a white shirt and a striped school tie. The two of them conversed as equals. Or, at least, the boy did. 'I understand how difficult it must be for you since daddy died, Mother. Don't worry about me; I am perfectly able to look after myself. You should marry Uncle Richard, he always brings me stuff.' The kid had to be from Oxenholme The Lake District!

'Shhhhhhh' his mother pleaded.

'Hey', Dave thought, 'I don't blame you lady. Just because you've been getting it on with good old Uncle Dick doesn't mean that you want to marry him! But how do you explain that to your precocious offspring?'

~

As constantly glancing at the yellow halter made him feel guilty, he tried staring at the reflection of it in the glass. Behind the breasts, the terrain was mostly farm country. He noticed that in Lancashire and Cumbria stone walls, not hedgerows, separated fields. Hay was yet to be harvested. Rows of cut grass lay in many fields, waiting baling and storing. In other fields, rolls of silage stood unwrapped. One thing all areas had in common, were the endless lines of power pylons.

The train stopped at Penrith and then Carlisle. Dave saw pretty villages with handsome houses made of the local stone. As they hurtled towards Scotland, he remembered how slow the trains of his youth had been compared with the express he now rode.

A group of elderly women got on the train at Motherwell. One of them unscrewed her warm and well-shaken bottle of pop and sprayed everyone in her vicinity with the sugary liquid.

~

With fifteen minutes of the journey remaining, people within range of the sprayed soda rose to clean themselves and, that done, prepare to get off the train. Doing so also afforded them a better look at the woman with the yellow halter.

One man called his significant other on his mobile phone. 'We just left Motherwell, so we'll be at Central Station within fifteen, hon. See you then.'

The halter woman almost ruined everything by speaking on her mobile 'phone. 'It's nay mah fuckin' fault we're late. Don't ya fuckin' take it out on me. Me an' the bairns had ta wait forever at Lancaster station.' She listened for a few seconds, then, 'Dinna fash yerself! We'll tek a taxi.' As she folded her 'phone away she noticed Dave looking at her. She shrugged her shoulders, tilted her head to one side and gave him a shy smile.

That was all the encouragement he needed. He rose from his seat and squeezed past passengers ready to alight. 'Hi. I've only got the one bag, so I come to offer my services as a porter for you and your girls. If you need one, that is.'

'Thankee, kind sir.' The woman smiled, inclined her head again and made as much of a mock curtsy as the confined space would allow. She knew what the head action did to men. The eldest daughter looked at Dave with unspoken malice. The younger continued to berate her doll for slurping its water. He tried to win the elder sibling's approval with a smile, realised the hopelessness of the act and reached for the items on the luggage rack. He put the assorted plastic bags on the table and the two suitcases on the floor in the aisle. A couple of passengers had to make room for the suitcases and they joined the eldest daughter in displaying their disapproval of Dave's actions and his motivation for them.

~

The train was fifty-three minutes late as it rolled into Glasgow Central. Dave picked up the two suitcases and headed for the door. 'I wonder if there's a budding Mussolini somewhere in this country,' he speculated.

'Who or what is a Mussolini when 'e's at home?' yellow halter asked.

'He was an Italian dictator whose only notable claim to fame was that he made the railways run on time.' Dave told her.

'Actually, that's nae true,' said the eldest daughter forcefully. 'Ma teacher told me Mussolini had a special train that he liked so much, he travelled everywhere in it. He only wanted his own train run on time, but then all the other trains had to keep to their timetables so as not to make his train wait.'

Dave smiled indulgently but felt like asking her if she understood the word, semantics.

Yellow halter carried Dave's bag and her handbag as the group made their way towards the ticket barrier. The girls carried the plastic bags. There was no ticket collector on duty and so Dave was able to lead the unhindered procession to the taxi rank. The driver helped stow the suitcases. Everything else went into the vehicle with the girls, leaving Dave and the woman alone on the pavement.

'My name's Dave,' he said as he extended his hand.

'Bonnie,' said the beauty as she put her hand in his.

'I'm only in Glasgow for a couple of days. Can I see you while I'm here? You could show me around.'

'Ah don't know. Ah've got a neurotic dog, two nosy and demanding parents, three dependent bairns and a boyfriend. Ah don't exactly have much time on me hands.'

'I guess tonight is out of the question then?' Dave said with a raised eyebrow.

'Ah'll have ta see. Here,' she opened her handbag and pulled out an eyebrow pencil and a pink tissue. She snapped the bag closed and used the side of it as a writing surface. 'Here's ma number. Give me a call later and Ah'll see how Ahm fixed. Okay?'

Dave grimaced at his recollection of the woman. She had told her parents to look after her children and her boyfriend believed she was seeing a friend, so she could spend two days with him. They had wined and dined, visited a cemetery and a cathedral. Bonnie was interested in architecture and had taken Dave to see many buildings she thought were impressive. However, most of the time was spent in Dave's hotel room where the woman's crude language and habits spoiled the fun for him. When the two days were finished, he was tired of the Scot and happy to leave. He crushed the tissue in his palm and dropped it in the bin.

Selective Reading

He picked up a dirty piece of white crumpled greaseproof paper that had a slight smell of fish about it. The fish man! Dave was surprised he had not already thrown the paper away. He rectified the situation. The fish man arrived at the pub most weekdays at around four in the afternoon with fresh fish wrapped in greaseproof paper and an outer covering of newspaper. He sold the fish to anyone who was interested, using the income to buy his beer. The man never allowed anyone to buy him a drink, as that presumably would lead to an established price for the fish. Dave had no idea what the man's name was or what he did for a living, but there was a stench of stale sweat and fish about him every day. The man would sit alone at a small table and stare out of the window, watching passing traffic in the street. He gathered newspapers abandoned by departing customers and, after consuming his usual four or five pints of bitter, would leave the pub with the newspapers tucked under his arm.

One day he had stayed late and consumed enough alcohol to become conversational. "Sold all me fish 'fore I got 'ere today. Sorry ya didn't 'ave the opportunity to buy some." He had ordered his seventh pint, causing Dave to worry that the man's malodorous presence might persuade some of the 'after-work' crowd to drink elsewhere. "I 'ope I'm not a pest. I like this pub." Dave had remained silent. "I'm Stephen Davies by the way. I think you know my Meredith." The man slid the piece of greaseproof paper across the bar. "Just call me if ever you and the missus want a nice piece of fish. Maybe the chef here would like to buy some one day."

Meredith Davies was the girl from the library who Dave had once dated.

~

He had been in the local library when a booming voice caused him to lift his head and pay attention.

"This disk was like this when we goddit 'ome. I even tried to clean it up some."

"I'm sorry, Mister Jackson, but that's our policy." The librarian was a mouth-watering vision of auburn-haired beauty. Her eyebrows were auburn. Even her freckles were auburn. She wore a single strand of pearls around her throat and pearl clip-on earrings. The olive-green pullover and sweater accentuated her shining hair.

"It was up to you to examine the CD before you left the library," she told the man in a cultured, husky voice.

"That's nonsense, lady. If you inspect every disk that's returned, why's it necessary for us to inspect 'em before taking 'em out?"

He had a point, but Dave decided he had to support the beauty.

"Well, unfortunately, we're not infallible."

I'll grant you infallibility, he'd thought, if that's what it takes. He'd wandered to a shelf of books, intending to select a couple that he could check out while the woman was still on duty.

"Neither am I, miss. Why don't we call it a draw?"

He stopped in mid-stride to watch and hear what happened next. The lovely librarian bit her bottom lip and re-inspected the disk.

A small girl pulled on the man's jacket. "Daddy, don't you remember…"

He brushed her hand away. "Not now, Suzie, there's a good girl."

The librarian put the disk in its holder and placed it under the counter. "We'll give you the benefit of the doubt this time, Mister

Jackson, but please take care of any disks you take out in future."

"Daddeeeee," the little girl insisted. "Remember…"

"I said not now, sweetheart. Daddy's busy."

The auburn-haired woman looked at the little girl and then, pointedly, at the father. Silence reigned. The librarian knew…Dave knew…everyone in the library knew the girl was privy to what had happened to the disk. And the father knew they all knew.

He coughed. "Well, that's it for now. I don't have time to take anythin' out; the wife's waitin' in the car."

He started to cross the room to the one-way electronic exit door. The big man strode and the little girl trotted past the silent, staring people who waited in line to check out books and compact disks. They'd passed within three feet of Dave.

"What're you looking at?" the man truculently demanded of him.

Dave had shrugged his shoulders. "Nothing."

The man had moved too quickly for his daughter and she had to run to keep up with him. "Mummy's not in the car, daddy. We left her at home with Mikey."

The man had said nothing. He increased his pace and the girl almost stumbled. "Wait for me, daddy."

The librarian had looked at her feet as she recovered from the experience. Dave instinctively knew it was the moment to strike. He reached out to the nearest rack and grabbed two books.

"You okay?" He asked her as he jumped the queue and reached the counter.

She raised her head and looked at him. "Me?" She even smiled. "Yes, I'm fine. Thank you."

Dave offered her the books and noticed she had no rings on her fingers. He took his wallet out of his pocket. "You often get situations like that?" He asked as he explored the dark spaces, looking for his library card.

"Only once in a blue moon." She looked at his books and smiled again. It had been time to ask her out for a drink. "How'd you…"

But she was already speaking. "Is your wife or girlfriend pregnant then?"

"What?"

"Your wife. Is she pregnant?"

"No, I…I'm not married."

"Your girlfriend then." The smile was still on her face, and in her eyes.

"No. I don't have a girlfriend." Dave had felt uncomfortable. "Why do you ask?"

She lowered her chin and raised her eyebrows. "These would seem to be books for an expectant father."

He looked at what he had picked off the shelf. 'What to Expect When You're Expecting' and 'Pregnancy After Thirty'. Expecting! He looked back at the delicious keeper of books.

"I, erm, look, er, when that man…could we go for a drink later?"

They had enjoyed just two dates before Meredith told him that, he being a barman and she a librarian, they weren't sociably suited for each other. Dave wondered why he had kept her father's number. He corrected his error.

A Useful Contact

A torn corner of a newspaper carried the number of one of the pub's two wheeler-dealers. Dave liked the brash young cockney who always seemed to have a deal cooking. Whenever the landlord needed something quickly, quietly, or cheaply, she always turned to the uninhibited guy. His latest offer was for delivery of cheap wrought-iron fencing. Danny claimed that during WWII, the government had asked people to dig up and surrender their iron fences for the war effort. Thousands of patriots had done as asked and the fences had been warehoused somewhere in the east-end of the city. The unutilised fencing was now reportedly available to anyone who wished to surround his or her property with a pre-war style garden enclosure. As Dave lived in a flat he had not taken advantage of the offer, but he might need such a street-wise person one day.

He entered Danny's name into the new diary.

Money for Nothing

Oliver Ponsonby's card could best be described as flamboyant. Dave had only known the well-groomed man for one eventful night. He had walked into the Coach House around nine o'clock having already consumed a considerable amount of alcohol.

"Evening, landlord. Gee and Tee with a twist, if you will."

"Certainly, but I'm not the landlord," Dave advised him. "Ice?"

"Good God, no. Do I look like an American? Ice only causes some of the good stuff to dissipate. Have one with me?"

"Thanks. I'll have a scotch, if that's okay."

The man paid for the drinks and sat on a barstool. "S'been a good day for me. Published me own book. They're finishing the printing of the first two-hundred copies as we speak. Nothing to shout about I know, but it's an achievement of sorts. Gives me a smattering of pride. Launching on Saturday. How'dya like to come and celebrate with me?"

"Tonight?" He nodded. "I don't know. I've gotta work 'til eleven thirty, quarter to twelve. You really want to wait until then?" Dave placed the man's change on the bar. "Where do you plan to go? What makes you think we'd hit it off?" The man picked up his drink and took a sip. Dave didn't know what to read into his cool lack of response. “Don’t you have any friends to celebrate with?”

The man returned his glass to the bar, making sure he placed it on the wet ring exposed when he picked it up. “My friends don’t like the book, so they don’t get to celebrate with me. Any man who serves alcohol to strangers has to be a fun guy and, uh, what else? Oh yes, let me say, right now, that I am not a poofter. Love the ladies. Go? Well, there’s a little club in the West End that can be quite droll. I can wait until you get off. What do ya say?” Dave hesitated and knew from the half-smile on the man’s face he was being assessed. “Take a chance,” the man urged.

“Maybe.” A free trip to the West End wasn’t too hard to take. “Let’s see how it goes.”

Dave took an order for a large round of drinks and left the writer to himself for a while. It seemed strange to even think of going to an unknown place with someone of whom he knew nothing. Yet, had the man had been a woman Dave knew he wouldn’t have given the matter a second thought. If the guy wanted to foot the bill, it could be fun.

“Another Gee and Tee, please. What’s your name, by the way?”

“Dave. Dave Wilson.” The two men shook hands. “Just one thing, I don’t have much money on me, working for a minimum wage has its limitations.”

“Oliver Ponsonby. Don’t worry about money, I’ve got oodles of the stuff. Whole thing is on me, plus a taxi home when we wrap it up. What do ya say?”

“Well, if you’re sure, okay.”

~

Dave was able to leave with his party-pal at eleven forty. Oliver summoned a passing taxi and gave the driver an address in the West End.

“What’s your book about?” Dave inquired.

“It’s one of those ‘how to’ books. ‘Making Money’, I’ve called it. I intend to advertise in magazines, newspapers and whatnot, telling prospective punters that for seven quid, plus postage and handling, they can learn how to make a fortune.”

“And how do you advise people to make said fortune?”

“Quite simple really. They just have to write a book telling others how to do it." Oliver laughed.

"But the people buying the book obviously don't know how to make money."

"I've just told them. Write a book telling people to write a book on how to make money."

"But you've already used up that idea."

"No, I don't think so. They just have to think up a new way of marketing the principle. One could advise readers to open up a petrol station, a fish and chip shop, or a grocery store. Don't have to tell them exactly how to do it."

Dave was incredulous. "Talk about money for nothing! Surely, that must be illegal."

"Not at all. I did some research into it and discovered that I can write just about anything I want. Mustn't give away state secrets or libel someone. Porno can get a bit iffy, but other than that, anything goes. Actually, it's damn-near a how-to on self-publishing but there are so many of those books about, I stuck to my original idea. I'm told I could have problems with the cover, though. I've printed a photograph of a twenty pound note on it and some legal chappie, who happened to be at the printers tonight, suggested it might give me a bit of a problem."

"What'll you do about that?" asked Dave.

"Nothing. I'll close me eyes and pray he's wrong. Spent too much money already, so I'll have to take me chances."

The taxi arrived at their destination. "Here we are, sir."

~

The 'West End' club turned out to be a second-story bar frequented by Jamaicans, many of whom wore the black, green and gold national colours and had Rastafarian dreadlocks. The room was full of smoke and very loud reggae music. There was marijuana in the air.

"Hey, mawwwwn. Where haaave you been?" People asked Oliver. "Welcome back." There were high fives, back slaps and hugs.

Oliver changed his drink to a single-malt whiskey and Dave saw no reason to complicate matters.

"Ah, the good stuff. This is a great place for a game of cricket."

"In here!"

"Absolutely. Do you play?"

"I turned out for the first eleven, but I'm not really any good."

"Doesn't matter. The idea is to have fun. The game here is played with a whiffle-ball. When they bring the grill down in front of the bar you'll know it's time to play. 'Til then have as much to drink as you want. Just tell my friend behind the bar, Mustafa, to put it on my tab.' He got Mustafa's attention and signalled that Dave's drinks be added to his tab. Try some of the ganja too, if you're inclined, that is."

"Is it good stuff?"

"It can be a killer. Varies a bit from night to night. Just take a couple of tokes at first and see how strong it is."

"What the hell is a, what did you call it, a whiffle ball?"

"You've never seen one?" Oliver was a little surprised. "It's a thin plastic ball with holes in it. Smack it as hard as you want but it won't go very far. Ideal for in here. Just keep your eye on your drink."

~

Friends gathered around and Oliver retold the tale of the book. "Bound to be a top ten seller. Let me buy you all a drink." He turned to the bar. "Mustapha! Give these good people a drink at my expense, would you. Have one yourself. There's a good fellow." People smiled indulgently and shook their heads at Oliver's social gaffs.

Dave circulated, looking to sample some ganja. He downed a couple of large Obans whilst joining in a conversation about cricket. The other people in the group knew far more about it than he did, so he wandered over to a collection of men and women who were discussing Bob Marley and smoking some powerfull smelling weed.

That Dave knew next to nothing about reggae music or Bob Marley didn't give him pause. "Hell of a song he wrote on the plane to London," he chimed in at a seemingly appropriate moment.

Conversation ceased for a full second.

"Whatchu on about, mawn?" asked one of the men.

"That song, 'I Can See Clearly Now', wasn't that by Marley?"

"Oh man, you cannot be fo' fucking real," laughed one of the females. "Here, stick this in your face and suck on it. You got to seriously lighten up."

Bingo! Dave drew deeply on the joint and sucked smoke into his lungs. He passed the joint on and held his breath for as long as possible. Eventually he had to let out the smoke but he did so as stingily as he could. The effect on his head and genitals was wonderful. The smiling Jamaican woman passed the joint to him a second time. "Have some mo' of da stuff that's good for what ails ya, mawn."

~

He went to the bar for another large Oban and returned to the group that was discussing cricket. The minutiae were now wondrous detail that enraptured Dave. He focused his attention on each speaker to make sure he caught every word. He had enough discipline to know if he started to talk he would ramble on for hours and so he opened his mouth only to sip the heavenly amber elixir held in his hand. He hadn't felt so good in a long time. He made a mental note to buy some of the grass before he left. He'd have to speak to Oliver about it. With luck, his host might even buy him an ounce.

~

The grill protecting the bar slid down with a bang. Dave jumped at the noise, almost spilling some of his whisky. He nearly gave himself whiplash as he spun his head around to see from where the sound had come. The noise in the room steadily ebbed until all conversation ceased. Two men donned white cricket sweaters over their clothes while others started to move the furniture against the walls. Everyone took the cue and joined in. Dave found he could handle two chairs back-to-back in his left hand whilst holding his glass in his right. Soon, the painted pitch which Dave had not previously noticed was cleared. Each man placed a heavy metal plate, on which were three white wickets, at opposite ends of the pitch. They then set about alternately selecting players for their respective teams. Neither of the captains even considered Dave. Once the teams were complete, the captains asked Oliver to officiate. A white fishing hat with a couple of lures attached and another white sweater appeared. Oliver tied the sleeves of the sweater around his waist so that the garment hung down behind him and placed the hat on his head.

~

Dave wandered over to the group that had been discussing Marley, hoping for another toke of ganja. He noticed that two of the men who had been in the group on his last visit were now playing cricket.

"Hey mawn. Were you shittin' us before?"

"Not really. I know Bob Marley's group was called 'The Wailers' but I don't actually know anything about him or reggae. I like Lennie Kravitz. Is that Reggae music?"

"Are you fo' real? Here, suck on this an' we'll see if it can get your white ass inta gear." Dave drew deeply on the spliff before passing it on. A batter hit the plastic ball sharply and drew Dave's attention to the game.

~

All bowlers were spinners and all used an underarm delivery. Dave was certain he could see the ball change direction in the air but then he considered how much mind-altering substance he'd imbibed and decided it wasn't something he wanted to discuss with anyone. The batters advanced down the wicket, taking wild swings at the ball before it hit the floor. Wicket keepers reached over the stumps, hoping the batter would miss the ball and not be able to return to the crease before the bails flew. Fielders took seemingly suicidal positions around the pitch. Most of them knelt on one knee with a drink at their feet and a joint or cigarette in their hand. Oliver made some controversial decisions that players sometimes questioned with vigour. Dave realised the arguments were for show and nobody really cared who won or lost. One fielder stopped a line drive with his left eye. Another one had the ball impaled on his index finger.

~

The game ended with a final score of 42 to 37. There was some heated discussion about how the score was calculated but, without a scoreboard, everyone had to accept Oliver's tally.

"How much you gettin' to let them win?" asked the losing captain.

"A figure of ten thousand pounds was mentioned, but I haven't seen the money yet," Oliver confessed with a grin.

Mustafa returned to his place behind the bar and raised the grill.

~

Oliver surrendered his badges of office and joined Dave. "Having a good time?"

"Yes, I am, thanks."

"You can stay here if you like but I have to go. Got to be up early to see a man about a dog. Here's twenty quid for a taxi. You can still drink on my tab. See you again in the Coach House."

~

The next day, Oliver appeared at lunch time. "Just dropped in to give you a copy of me book. There's an inscription on the fly page. You never know, signed first editions have been known to fetch a couple of shekels at auction. I'll give you me card, as well. Next time you fancy a trip up West, give me a call. Other than that, I'll see you now and then,"

~

Dave never saw the man again.

Five months later, on a quiet afternoon, he idly scanned the pages of an Evening Standard abandoned by a departed customer. Buried in the middle, he came across a brief report about a man sentenced to a year in prison. He had improperly reproduced the image of a twenty-pound note on the cover of a book. Authorities had recovered and destroyed one-hundred and seventy-seven copies.

Dave remembered Oliver's words about a run of 200 copies and realised he owned one of the twenty-three unrecovered books. How many of the others, he wondered, had a personalised inscription in them? Maybe the book would be worth something in two or three decades. He remembered the comment he had made when he understood what Oliver's book was about; money for nothing. He'd gone to the office, picked up a pair of scissors and cut around the article, ensuring he captured the date.

At home, Dave had slipped the article inside the cover of the book he had almost thrown away. He smiled as he again read the inscription. *To my kind friend, Dave Wilson - a man who serves alcohol to strangers.*

He looked to his bookcase to confirm the book still stood in place, then at the card of *Oliver Ponsonby, Author and Adjudicator.* He smiled as he crossed the room to the bookcase and inserted the card into the pages of the book.

The Prize

Kate's kiss. He held the piece of paper that bore the imprint of her lips and recalled their time together. The reputation of the Coach House had never been better and thus business was booming. Consequently, the owner awarded permanent employees a two-week job-swap-experience with workers at a bar she part-owned in New York City called the Inn Famous. When Dave flew to 'the Big Apple' in September, Ellen had already made the trip and he had ready-made friends waiting for him.

Once he passed through Immigration and Customs, he exited the British Airways terminal to wait for a specially marked Holiday Inn courtesy bus that was to take him to his Manhattan lodgings. The scene outside the automatic glass doors seemed to be total chaos. He saw taxis, limousines, private cars, car-hire buses, line buses, hotel courtesy buses, baggage trolleys, baggage and a lot of people queuing for buses and taxis or anxiously looking around for whoever was to pick them up. Small, brown men in orange and yellow tabards tried to control traffic but were ignored by all. Horns blared and whistles blew

Dave stopped a bus with the Holiday Inn motif painted on it. 'Sorry sir, but you'll have to wave down the one that belongs to the city hotel. I'm only taking people to the airport hotel.'

It took another thirty minutes for Dave's bus to arrive and he became a little agitated as the long minutes ticked by.

~

On his first day at the bar, inappropriately named Inn Famous, Dave was to start work at ten in the morning. He left the hotel early, as he was unsure how long it would take him to walk to his destination. It wasn't hard to find the place where he would work for the next two weeks. The system of numbered streets made finding Thirty-Ninth Street an easy task. He'd learned from someone at the hotel that Lexington Avenue was on the East Side of the city, so he walked east on thirty-ninth until he found the corner where the bar was situated. He arrived at twenty to ten and had to wait for fifteen minutes before someone arrived to open the door. The man with the keys introduced himself as Andy. After Andy switched on the lights and air-conditioning, he asked Dave to restock the bar, clean the tables and get to know other staff members as they arrived. Andy left an hour later, stating that he turned up each morning solely to open the place and to pick up the previous day's receipts.

~

The lunch trade was not impressive, but staff assured Dave that 'Attitude Adjustment Hour', which stretched from four-thirty to seven, as well as the late shift, were going to be more than a 'Brit. barkeep' could handle. For rest of the day, Dave learned how to make some of the complicated cocktails that many of the clientele liked to imbibe.

When his shift was over at four-thirty, Dave transferred himself to the consumer's side of the bar and watched his temporary co-workers in action. Regular customers were aware of the reason for Dave's visit and many of them bought him 'Welcome to the good old U. S. of A.' drinks. Many female customers engaged Dave in conversation just so they could listen to his British accent.

One woman, who hailed from New Zealand, took the stool next to Dave and they quickly became friends. She was, she advised him, waiting for her employer and a couple of workmates. Her employer owned a travel agency, he, and all the staff were ex-patriots from the land of the kiwi. Unfortunately, Dave had to return to his hotel room, before the others arrived as he was feeling the effects of jet lag and several large drinks. He told the friendly blonde lady, Marianne, that he was working the four to midnight shift the following day and he hoped to see her then.

The next day, the staff allowed Dave to serve drinks to customers. He learned to count the numbers of drinks customers purchased and provided every fourth one as a gift 'on the house' or 'buy-back'. He enjoyed being treated with respect by the American customers and marvelled at the tips he was given. It occurred to him that if some of the mean, tight-fisted Brits who drank at the Coach House had to give such generous tips, they would probably stop drinking. Dave noticed that whenever staff heard an English accent on the other side the bar, nobody rushed to serve its owner. He initially thought that the staff was allowing him to talk to a fellow countryman until the Brits departed without leaving a tip. His Yankee buddies saw no reason to serve someone who didn't believe that the server was at least their equal and deserving of some tangible appreciation.

Marianne appeared during 'Attitude Adjustment Hour' when, instead of the house buying every fourth drink, there was a 'two-for-one' offer in effect. Dave served her a 'Cuba Libra' and marked her cocktail napkin to indicate he owed her a second drink. A short time later, three people joined her. Marianne made introductions as he placed each beverage in front of each newcomer.

Ivor had a vodka martini. 'Pleased to meetcha. Marianne says you're over here on some sort of prize. Seems a shame you have ta work.'

'Hi. It's not so bad. It's a cheap way of seeing New York and meeting new people.'

Sheila drank a Manhattan 'on the rocks', 'Not too much sweet Vermouth please. Where are you staying?'

'The Holiday Inn on Seventh Avenue,' Dave told her.

'God. That hell hole. Keep well away from the ladies there.'

Kate had a bottle of Becks, 'I'm straight and simple but I have to pee a lot.'

'Just as long as you use the bathroom,' Dave laughed.

'Same again, please,' said Marianne. Dave gave her a fresh drink and a new napkin.

~

The crowd thinned out once the 'twofers' stopped at seven o'clock and Dave got to spend more time speaking to the New Zealanders.

'When do you next work the first shift?' Ivor wanted to know.

'Friday, I think. These guys seem to like me, but they're not about to give up the big tips earned on Friday night.'

'Can't blame them for that. How about we take you out on Friday and show you the town?'

'That would be great. Thanks.'

'It's a date. I have to go back to the office now but I'm in and out of this place all the time, so I'll fill you in on the details later.' Ivor finished his drink. 'Come on you three. There's plenty of work still to be done.'

Dave thanked them and put the twenty-dollar tip in the pint pot behind the bar, along with the money earned by others working the same shift.

Kate returned just before eleven and sat on a vacant stool at the far end of the bar.

'Becks?' Dave asked.

'It'll do for now. How's it going? Made many fuck-ups?'

'This one's on me. Just the one. Some idiot asked for a gin and tonic and when I served it he swore he asked for a vodka and tonic. I think he's done it before because all the manager wanted to know, was how much of the drink had the man drunk before he decided he'd been served the wrong beverage?'

'New York is full of assholes like that.'

'Did you get your work finished?' Dave inquired. He wasn't interested in the answer but he did want to keep the conversation going. Kate was a good-looking woman. He estimated her height to be five-nine or ten. She was big boned and big breasted with brown shoulder length wavy hair and challenging green eyes. She wore very little make up and no jewellery. The Kiwi sat cross-legged on the stool and the relatively low bar afforded Dave a glimpse of an exposed and well-shaped thigh. Other customers required Dave's attention and while he was serving them he noticed a man take a seat next to Kate.

The man called him over. 'Let me have a large scotch on the rocks, will ya? How about you?' he asked of Kate.

'I'm fine, thank you.'

'You Sure? My name's Kurt. You?'

'Kate.'

'Hey, ain't that somethin'; Kate and Kurt. We must be meant for each other.'

Dave put the man's drink in front of him. 'That'll be four fifty please.'

Kate told the man, 'I hardly think so.'

The man threw a five-dollar bill on the bar. 'Keep the change.' He turned his attention back to Kate, 'Why on earth not?'

'I'm waiting for my friend Dave, here, to finish his shift and then we're going to leave together.'

Dave experienced a rush of elation and knew that the grin on his face must have looked school boyish. He picked up the money and walked back to the cash register. When he turned back he saw that the man had risen and was shaking Kate's hand.

'I hope I didn't cause any offence.' He polished off his drink and left the bar.

Dave finished his shift on the stroke of midnight. He walked through the bar's gate and Kate rose from her stool. As he fell into step alongside the Kiwi, she slipped her arm under his and squeezed his bicep. 'Come on home, my Limey friend. Let me show you some good old New York hospitality.'

A business commitment meant Ivor had to postpone Friday's night out. He promised they would do something special a week later. That Friday would be Dave's last night in New York and so everyone thought that it was the appropriate time for a big bash in his honour. Kate and Dave spent the rest of their free time between her apartment and his hotel room. The boss and employees of Travel Tix & Tours hopped in and out of Inn Famous at all hours of the day and night. They had lunch and sometimes dinner at the bar. Cash never changed hands, except for the generous tips that Ivor always left. Andy told Dave that he sent the bill to Ivor on a weekly basis.

~

Kate took Dave to see the New York Mets play baseball on Saturday afternoon. The almost tasteless, gassy lager that Dave drank did nothing to relieve the heat and humidity. After three enormous plastic coated paper cups of the liquid, Dave decided to try a hot-dog, or 'frank' as Kate called it. The sausage was about eight inches long. Kate insisted that he smear American mustard and some chopped green stuff on his dog. It was surprisingly good. Dave downed more of the beer and ordered another 'frank'. They stayed in the corridor behind the stands and queued up ('stood in line' is how Kate put it) to buy two more beers, finishing their old ones as they waited. Once they had their beers in one hand and a frank in the other, they headed back to their seats. They heard the crack of a bat against the ball and the resultant roar of the crowd. The two hurried up the narrow incline that led to their seats, trying not to spill their beer. People who had been about to enter the corridor stopped and turned back to watch the action on the field below.

'What happened?' Kate asked.

'The Kid hit a solo,' one man informed her.

'What's a solo?' Dave asked.

'A home run with no-one on base. Only one run scored – a solo.'

'Okay. So, what's the score now?'

'Two to one Mets with three innings to go,' the man said.

The pair retook their seats amongst the happy supporters. People were slapping each other's palms and grinning.

'You two missed a monster from The Kid. Hit the ball clean outa the park behind the Mets' bullpen.'

Dave didn't bother to ask what a bullpen might be doing in a baseball stadium, but Kate read his mind. 'The bullpen is the area where relief pitchers warm up.'

There were no more runs scored by either side so Dave and Kate were with a happy crowd as they filed out of the stadium.

~

Eversall, one of the bar staff at the Inn Famous, offered to take Dave to his local pub on the Sunday to watch a football game.

'That'd be great. Thanks. Who's playing?'

'Jets versus a bunch of mutts collectively known as the Giants. They're both New York teams but they play in different leagues. The Giants, a New York team though they be, play their games in the swamps of New Jersey. Every now and then, the schedule includes inter-league games between local rivals.

'As the Giants are the mutts, I gather you must support the pedigree Jets?'

'Damn straight! I figure you'll be rooting for them too, seeing as how you'll be my guest.' Eversall's smile took the edge off his words.

'Of course. Isn't New Jersey a different state?'

'It is. New Jersey is the state next to this one, just across the Hudson River. The Giants used to play in New York but they moved to a great new stadium in New Jersey. The rubes from New Jersey think the team belongs to them now because they dropped the letters NY from their name. We arrogant New Yorkers know differently.'

'But, if you're a Jet fan, why do you care?'

'Once a New Yorker, always a New Yorker, especially in sports.'

~

The pub where they were to watch the game had eighteen television sets. Three behind the bar, six suspended from the ceiling, four on shelves around the room, four others over doorways and one recessed in the ceiling, 'for those who are falling-down-drunk'. Before the game started, different sets showed different sporting events. Some live, others recorded. There was baseball, soccer, surfing, fishing, car racing, track and field, rugby and even Australian Rules football. At one o'clock, all sets switched to the Jets versus Giants game. The Jets were favoured by two and a half points but the mostly Jet crowd seemed to agree that the margin would be greater in a low scoring game.

'Why the half point?' Dave asked.

'To make sure there's a result for the gamblers.'

Eversall's cousin-in-law, Jeff joined the two men after the start of the game. He was a Giants' fan but freely admitted the Jets would probably win the game. The three sat together in the middle of the bar. One television directly in front of them and, should something happen to that set, another at each side. They could also see a reverse angle shot on other television screens reflected in the mirror behind the bar. They ignored the screen in the ceiling.

Free food seemed to appear every thirty minutes or so. Chips (fries), slices of pizza, miniature hot-dogs and small hamburgers. The three barmen worked hard to meet the constant demand for pints of beer. The chant 'Jets Jets Jets' rang out whenever that team possessed the ball. Whenever the Giants had the ball, 'Deefence - deefence' was heard followed immediately by,' Jets Jets Jets'. The consumption of beer increased. Glasses and bottles were banged on the bar and table tops; feet stomped to the chant of 'Jets Jets Jets.' More people crowded into the relatively small pub. The air was full of cigarette smoke and the alcohol was taking its effect. 'Jets Jets Jets.'

The Giants won the game 41 points to 28.

~

On Monday evening, Kate and Dave went to a pub called 'The Quiet Little Table in the Corner' for dinner. Their quiet little table, like the others in the dark place, turned out to be a booth. They downed several drinks before ordering their food. During scarce moments when they weren't concentrating on each other, they noticed two women sitting in the booth opposite them. Kate adjudged the pair to be 'out-of-towners in the city for some shopping and a couple of shows'. One of the women slid out of her seat, presumably to visit the bathroom. Kate asked Dave what impressions of New York he would relate to friends and colleagues when he returned to Yuck.

'*Yuck*?' Dave repeated.

She laughed. 'Isn't that how it's pronounced? You know, the U and the K for United Kingdom. If not, then it should be.'

'Really? Well, I'll be telling them they should look for Kiwis because you lot give it up in no time flat.'

'Oh yeah,' said Kate as she lightly stabbed him in the back of his hand with her fork. 'You do that and I'll fork you to death.'

The woman from the opposite table had chosen the moment to return and she nearly gave herself whiplash when she misheard Kate's remark. She sat down on the edge of the booth's semi-circular seat, trapping the tablecloth under her thigh. As she slid towards the centre of the leather bench, the tablecloth slid with her. Her half-full glass of water tipped over and a couple of pieces of cutlery dropped to the carpet. She quickly reversed the movement, freed the burgundy-coloured material, mopped up the water with her napkin and put everything back in its place. When she was satisfied everything was as it should be, she carefully moved closer to her friend. The pair joined and lowered their heads as she quickly told her tale. A few seconds later, both heads rose simultaneously and the women stared at Dave and Kate.

'Hi.' Kate smiled at the pair.

The women looked down at their table's surface. One of them fiddled with a strand of pearls at her throat. The other pushed some food around her plate.

~

Kate borrowed a friend's car on Tuesday and took Dave for a combined trip of sightseeing and shopping. They drove over a bridge and out of Manhattan, through the streets of Brooklyn, then returned along the Eastern shore of the bay and passed under the Verrazano Bridge. On their left, cargo ships rode at anchor and to the right of the vessels stood the twin towers of the World Trade Center. As they passed one ship, the green coloured Statue of Liberty came into view. Dave took photographs. They re-entered Manhattan via the Brooklyn/Battery tunnel and drove up the West Side of the city, thereby allowing Dave to take some shots of the Lady of Liberty from a different angle. Kate parked the car under the World Trade Center and they took the lift up one-hundred-and-eight floors to a restaurant aptly named Windows of The World. Three German businessmen rose with them in the elevator. One of them took a fob watch from his waistcoat pocket and timed their ascent, nodding his approval as they sped upward through the core of the building.

Kate told the maitre d' (whom she obviously knew) that they were not staying to eat but she wanted only to show the views to her friend from overseas. The man nodded his assent and greeted the three Germans. Kate took Dave's arm and led him on a circuit of the restaurant. They looked down on the ships that appeared like toys beneath them. The Statute of Liberty appeared no larger than

Dave's thumbnail. On the opposite side of the building, the city of Manhattan stretched out before them. Traffic wound along avenues, looking like lines of ants. Dave was impressed.

There were other sights, but it became clear to Dave that the sightseeing was merely foreplay for Kate's shopping. She called out certain landmarks. 'This is the meat market; actual meat during the day and hangouts for gays at night.'

They sped past the 'QE II' and the USS 'Enterprise' but Kate was in no mood to stop.

She parked the car and they entered a store named 'Bloomindales'. Kate headed straight for the handbag department, where a sale was going on. Her initial pleasure at seeing the sea of handbags turned to frustration as she was unable to find one she wanted. She rejected many as being over-priced, too squishy, too formal, too big, too small, good, but not quite right, too fancy, wrong colour, poorly finished, scuffed or stained. She kept going back to inspect a couple of bags, but in the end none of them measured up to her standards.

Back on the street, they headed south on foot and Kate feigned surprise at finding another store selling handbags. A quick inspection showed that none of them was up to scratch but the boots were interesting. Seven pairs later, she had a winner. Well, maybe. She tried on the right boot and then took it off. She tried on the left one. She tried them both on. She stood for a long time in front of an angled mirror, turning to her right and left. The knee-length black boots were unzipped and re-zipped. She made three more circuits of the store.

'Do you think they're okay?' she asked Dave.

'They're bloody marvellous,' he begged her to accept. 'In any case, if you don't take them off soon, the store will tell you you've worn them for so long that they're yours whether you want them or not.'

'That's silly,' Kate smiled.

Then she checked the price. Dave silently exploded. How could she have spent so long in trying them out, if she hadn't checked to see if they were in her price range?

'Not so bad. A hundred dollars marked down from one hundred

and fifty. And there's a further twenty per cent off. That makes them eighty dollars. What do you think?'

'I think they're great. Now let's pay for them and get out of here.'

The pimply man at the counter made his calculations, 'That'll be fifty-two fifty,' he advised Dave. Kate thumped Dave's thigh to ensure he remained silent.

'Dave, that was great,' Kate exploded once they were on the pavement – or sidewalk. That was also very kind of you to pay for them. That wasn't what I had intended.'

'I know.' Dave smiled. 'I had to get you out of there before you corrected the man's calculations. You looked like you were about to spill the beans.'

~

That night, Kate told Dave he should wear something special for Friday, but refused to tell him why he should do so. She inspected his wardrobe and declared he needed a new Italian suit plus a shirt and tie. His socks would suffice but he needed a new pair of shoes. Kate insisted they go to Barney's the next day where she would charge everything on her American Express card.

'I am capable of buying my own clothes, thank you,' Dave insisted.

'I'm sure you are but this is something I want to do. I want to dress my man to match my Friday outfit. The night is not just about you.'

The salesman reasoned Dave could not have socks worthy of the new outfit, so he threw in a pair free of charge.

'Thank you, but I must tell you my socks would have been satisfactory. They're part of my uniform.'

The man gaped at Dave, 'Uniform?'

'Yes. I work behind a bar in London.'

'You're a lawyer?'

'Not exactly,' Kate advised the effeminate man. 'More of a mixologist.'

'Oh, *that* kind of bar.'

~

Kate convinced Dave to try on his new purchases once they were back in his hotel room.

'You are one handsome man', she told him. 'Well worth every cent. You'd better look after those shoes, though. They cost a fortune.'

'How much do I owe you?' Dave asked.

'Not a dime. This is my gift. Come Friday, we're having a whole bunch of photographs taken and my pleasure will be in seeing you in this getup long after you've gone back to Yuck and forgotten all about me.'

'Well, firstly, thank you very much and, secondly, I don't think I'll ever forget you.'

'Yes you will. Your memory will probably fade at the same rate that these shoes wear out.'

'That'll be a long time. These are good shoes.'

'Yes they are. And I'm here to tell you that they must not ever, and I mean ever, be worn behind a bar.'

'They won't be. Thanks again for buying all this stuff. It must have cost a small fortune.'

'It did, so why don't you come over here and try showing me how much you appreciate it.'

~

Kate tried to cut Dave's hair on the Wednesday night but as they were both naked at the time she only got half of the job done and so he had to visit a barber's shop the following day.

~

After work on Friday, Dave went back to his hotel room with Kate.

She was already wearing a black cocktail dress that displayed her beautiful cleavage and wore a single strand of pearls at her throat. Dave shaved and showered before putting on his new clothes.

'Oh Lord, those clothes do maketh my man,' Kate enthused. 'It's a pity we don't have a little more time.'

~

They took a taxi to the Waldorf Astoria to meet Ivor, Marianne and Sheila for a drink. Ivor was dressed in a charcoal grey suit, blue shirt with a white collar and a military looking tie. He was refilling the glasses of his two seated employees.

'Here they are. Now my entourage is complete. You look ravishing as usual, my lovely Kate.' He caught the attention of a waiter. 'Would you bring me two more glasses and another bottle of this bubbly.'

Kate sat down whilst Dave went to receive a kiss of greeting from the other two ladies. Sheila was wearing a cream coloured dress that adequately covered her chest but to which he could not see a back. A tiara-like-fastener held the hair she had piled high on her head. Marianne wore a red dress with sparkling sequins. She also wore gloves of the same colour that almost reached her arm-pits.

~

Dave sat down next to Kate and she rubbed lipstick from his cheek. Ivor poured the pair a glass each of the champagne before raising his own glass.

'To Sir Keith Holyoke. Here's to another term in office.' Marianne suppressed her laughter but was having difficulty getting the words out.

Dave swallowed his champagne too quickly and it burned its way down his throat.

'Sir Keith Holyoke!' He laughed out loud.

'I will thank you to show a little more respect for my office,' cautioned Ivor.

'I'm terribly sorry your honour.'

'That's more like it.'

Dave took another sip of champagne, 'What's happening here?'

Kate leaned across the space between their chairs, 'I thought it must be nice for celebrities and their ilk to dine at The Four Seasons. Then I figured that nobody in New York has any idea who our one-time Prime Minister was or how old he would be now, never mind what he looks like. I couldn't make reservations, in case someone thought of checking into Sir Keith's details. We're going to ask for a reservation when we are in the limo and pray to God that they can squeeze us in. We ordered a limo for seven forty five. Think you can help us carry it off?'

'Hell, yes.'

Ivor topped-up everyone's glass. 'Drink up everyone, it's time to leave.'

As they walked out of the hotel, Dave saw that Sheila's dress was cut extremely low in the back.

~

Once in the limousine, Kate produced her mobile 'phone, cautioned her companions to be quiet, and called the restaurant to advise them that Sir Keith Holyoke was on his way and could they possibly find a table for him and his four guests. As hoped, the establishment would be happy and honoured to have Sir Keith grace them with his presence.

Two busboys and a supervisor were still laying the red carpet as the limousine pulled up. Another party of diners stepped onto the carpet and was about to ascend the steps to the front door when the supervisor discouraged them.

He shook an extended finger to and fro, 'Ladies and gentlemen, *please*!'

~

The driver stopped at exactly the right spot, got out of the vehicle and hurried around to open the door for his very important passenger. Ivor stepped onto the carpet and the poor driver was so impressed, he lowered his head in reverence. The others followed Ivor and mounted the steps. Dave fought the laughter trying to erupt from his chest. He gave himself and the others an excuse to release their suppressed laughter.

'That was a hell of a joke, Sir Keith. It seems even funnier now it has sunk in.' The release was wonderful and they laughed their way past the supervisor who dutifully held the front door of the restaurant open for them.

Ivor turned back to the man, 'Nice touch with the carpet. Thank you very much. I appreciate it.' He gave the man forty dollars.

The Maitre D' escorted them to a table where five white-gloved staff waited to assist them in seating. The staff then smartly snapped open the starched white napkins and placed them on the diners' laps.

Instead of opening the wine list, Ivor surveyed his party. 'I think we've all agreed to drink nothing but champagne tonight. Two bottles of the '88 Taittinger Brut Reserve now and then just keep the stuff coming. Thank you.'

The menus didn't display prices, but it did read very well. All had a five-course meal that was incredibly good. Ivor paid the bill in cash as a cheque or credit card would have given away his identity. Thankfully, he had been to the bank during the day and was prepared to pay whatever the bill totalled. The limousine was waiting as they left the restaurant. Someone had rolled up the red carpet.

~

The driver stopped at the Inn Famous and the group walked into the crowded bar. 'Here he is!' someone called out.

'All right Dave, ma main *man*,' shouted Eversall as he presented Dave with a tee shirt that read:

HONORARY LIFETIME MEMBER
BARKEEPING CORPSE
'INN FAMOUS'
NEW YORK, NY

The champagne hardly measured up to the Taittinger but it was just as enjoyable. Dave shook hands and hugged everyone behind the bar as well as three others who had come in on their night off just to say goodbye.

The group went to Ivor's apartment to continue the party. Fifteen minutes later, Sheila's boyfriend Sean, who had just finished work at one of the brokerage houses, joined them.

'Did you bring any champers?' his girlfriend asked of him.

'No, but I do have some nice grass.'

'Grass! I am shocked,' cried Marianne. 'Do you have rolling papers?'

'Does the Pope live in Rome?'

'Good man,' said Sheila, 'Give them here and let me roll a joint or three'

Marianne went into the bedroom and re-emerged with the game of Trivial Pursuit. The six split into three boyfriend/girlfriend teams and spent more than two hours playing the game whilst depleting Ivor's stock of champagne and smoking the marijuana. Twice, there erupted heated but friendly discussions on whether the answers given to questions agreed with the answers on the cards.

~

Arlene was the first person from Inn Famous to arrive at around two thirty,

'The place is pretty dead now. Eversall and Jackie will be here in a minute. Mike'll close the place up.'

'Aren't you tired?' Dave asked. 'What the hell are you doing here?'

'Ivor told us all to come round; something to do with a literal last fling. Ask him.'

Dave looked at the grinning Ivor.

'We're all going to Coney Island for a ride on the Cyclone – that's the Big Dipper to you.'

'Are you kidding?'

'Not at all!'

The bell rang and Ivor spoke into the intercom to tell Eversall and Jackie to wait downstairs. The men grabbed their jackets and the women put on their shoes. The limousine still waited and nine bodies managed with comparative ease to squeeze into the stretched version of a Lincoln Continental. Kate sat on Dave's lap and tried her best to make him uncomfortable.

~

When the car arrived at Coney Island, they found the place almost deserted. The rides had long since shut down. The Lincoln found its way to the side of the Cyclone and they all got out. A man dozing in one of the ride's carriages awakened at the group's arrival.

'Sorry to have kept you waiting,' apologised Ivor.

'S'allright. This all your party then?'

'Yes. Just keep the thing going round until I yell for you to stop, Okay?'

'S'okay by me, but I think you're all nuts. You got the cash?'

'Five hundred dollars, right,' said Ivor and handed the man the money.

Ivor reserved the front seat for himself and Marianne. Sheila and Sean were next, then Dave and Kate. Eversall sat between Arlene and Jackie, one arm around each set of shoulders. The operator released the brake and the car started its long climb to the top of the first crest.

The slumbering rides of the fairground provided no artificial light and so, as they slowly climbed to the first summit, the only illumination was that of the new moon. They could see the parallel rails in front of them and the stripe of moonlight on the water in the bay. The only sound in the night was the click, click, click of the chain that pulled their carriage up the steep slope. As the front of the coach started to dip down to reveal the steepness of the descent, Marianne let out a scream that pierced the relative silence of the night.

'Holy fucking shit. Stop this thing now!'

'No can do lover,' laughed Ivor as they started to plunge downward.

The sight also impressed Kate. 'Holy mother of God,' she said, before burying her face in Dave's chest. The carriage whipped itself through the 'U' at the base of the loop and then started its tortuous climb up the next incline. Much to Sean's dismay, Sheila stood up and freed the top of her dress, exposing her breasts to the night air. She completed the manoeuvre before Sean had the time to object.

As they neared the crest of the next hill, Ivor turned in his seat. 'Everyone must raise their arms in the air as we go down this time,' he ordered.

'Go down!' screamed Marianne. 'I'll never go down on you again, you lousy prick. Let me off this thing now.'

'Sorry, dear, no can do.'

Round and round they went. A few stomachs felt a little queasy, but nothing violent happened. After several circuits, a couple of people started to feel confident and that, combined with the influence of champagne and grass, encouraged them to take risks.

The operator stopped the ride as they passed his station. 'If any o youse do anytin' stupid, I'll toss ya off da ride. Unnerstand?'

'That's okay, 'cause I want off right now,' Marianne shouted as she pushed up the safety bar and wrestled herself free of Ivor grasp. 'I'll wait for you in the car.'

They went around a couple of more times, but the fun had gone and so Ivor signalled the operator to stop the ride.

Once they were in the vehicle, Marianne was happy to see them.

'That was a hell of a way to finish the night and my visit to America,' said Dave. 'Thanks.'

'It isn't over yet as far as you and I are concerned,' breathed Kate. 'Can I have tomorrow, or I should say today, off, boss?' she asked of Ivor.

'Seeing as it's Saturday, I think that can be arranged.'

The limousine dropped people off at their respective dwellings. When they got to Kate's apartment, Dave thanked Ivor once again. 'I've never had so much fun on one night. If you come to Blighty, you've got to let me know and we'll get together again. Bye.'

~

After a robust romp, Dave asked Kate if it was likely that she would go to England.

'I might.'

He sensed hesitation and was a little hurt. 'You make it sound like you wouldn't let me know, even if you did go.'

'Look Dave, we've had twelve great days together. It's not as if we're to become engaged or something. I might want to finish things between us once you get on the plane this evening. I'm not sure right now and I might not be sure until the prospect of a trip to London presents itself.'

'Well I'd sure as hell like to see you again.' Dave picked up Kate's address book and wrote his name, London address and telephone number in it. Then he turned to the back of the book and tore out one of the pages reserved for notes, went over to Kate's 'phone, lifted it off the hook and copied her number on the piece of paper. As he turned back to Kate, he saw that her eyes had welled up with tears.

'Don't be hurt or mad Dave, we've had a wonderful time together. Why can't we leave it at that? It could be months before we have the opportunity to see each other again and I don't want to lead a celibate existence until then. I'm sure that you don't either.'

Dave looked at the woman he had come to love, but he'd be damned if he was going to tell her that now. 'It's not the way I'd have things, but if that's what you want I guess there is nothing I can do about it.'

After tender sex, they took a taxi to the Holiday Inn where Kate helped Dave pack his bags. Ivor had kindly arranged for a different limousine to take them to the airport. Once Dave had checked in, the two lovers went to a bar for a farewell drink. They kissed goodbye and then Kate handed him an envelope.

'You can only open this after the plane has taken off,' she said. 'Promise?'

'Promise.'

~

The stewardess announced the captain had turned off the 'fasten seatbelts' sign. Dave thought he'd waited long enough so he took the envelope from his jacket pocket and ripped it open. Inside was a piece of paper with the imprint of a mouth. Kate must have kissed the paper.

'I have loved you but now it's time for you to go. Take care of yourself and be happy.'

~

When Dave got back to his flat, he put the paper with Kate's 'phone number in his diary. He had intended to call her at some future time to see if she'd had second thoughts, but somehow he never got around to it.

The trip had been well over a year ago. Other than receiving copies of the photographs of his final night in New York, there had been no contact between himself and anyone from the travel agency. He had sometimes worn the tee shirt when working a Saturday lunch, but telling the story behind it had become tiresome and the garment now lay at the bottom of a drawer. There no longer seemed to be a point in keeping Kate's address and phone number. He smiled and hoped Kate was as well and happy as he was with Jane in his life.

Good to The Last Drop

One quiet lunch-time Brian Carter stretched his hand across the bar. 'We know each other's names but we don't really know each other, do we?'

Dave took his hand and smiled. 'You're a gee-and-tee with a twist to me.'

'Exactly. I call myself The Silver Fox. I'll grant it's a tad theatrical but people remember the name and that's what I want them to do. I'm a buyer, seller, and fixer. You have anything to trade, I'm your man.'

Dave had heard Carter claim to have been educated at Britain's best schools but he also had more than his share of street smarts. 'Well, I'm sorry to say all I have to sell is booze and you already know that.'

'Yes. Thing is, I notice people talk to you. If ever someone tells you they've invented something or have an heirloom to sell, I want you to tell them to talk to me. If I take them on, I'll make it worth your while. I take ten per cent as my fee and I'll give you ten per cent of that, minimum twenty quid. What do you say?'

'All right. You got a card?'

Bryan was usually in the company of entertaining people who

spent money freely and often left generous tips. Several of them rented a house each summer somewhere near the New Forest. There, they spent the weekdays entertaining friends, lonely wives, business associates, and party-pals. The wheeler/dealer sometimes took prospective clients to the retreat, where he or she could meet business contacts.

~

Sergei Rabinovitz was an untidy, bookish man and an occasional drinker who kept to himself. His hair looked like black and grey wire. He was always dressed in well-worn canvas pants, a blue denim shirt and a chunky woollen sweater. The man would come into the pub with a newspaper tucked under his arm, order a pint of Guinness and then retreat to a table in the corner of the room where he would read and slowly sip his stout. He always bought a second pint, but never a third. Rumour in the pub was that Sergei, together with his siblings and parents had somehow escaped from German occupied Warsaw during WWII.

One Tuesday in May, Sergei drank at the bar.

'Not sitting at your table today?' Dave asked.

'No, not today.'

Dave stuck a wooden toothpick between his teeth. 'You need to chat?'

The man took a sip of his pint. He opened his mouth, took a breath and then closed it.

'Is your pint okay?'

'Yes. You always pour a good pint of Guinness in this pub. That is why I come here.'

'Did you walk here? It looks nice outside.'

'Yes, I walked. I always walk.'

'So what do you do?'

'Sorry? I do not understand. What I do?'

'Yeah. What do you do? Work? How do you earn your daily crust?'

'Oh. Yes. I see. Well, actually I am the custodian at the block of flats just down the road from here. It is called Greene Mansions. Do you know it?'

'Yeah. I walk past it twice a day.'

'Yes,' Sergei responded.

Dave was unsure if the man was correcting his English or making what seemed to be an odd observation. 'Married?'

'Me? No. I live alone in the basement of Greene Mansions.'

'No windows, eh?'

'Yes. No window is correct. One of my reasons for coming here for a drink is to get out into the open air. I don't mind the kind of weather. A walk in the rain is sometimes just as pleasant as a walk in the sunshine, which is a good thing for somebody who lives in England.' A smile appeared on Sergei's face, and then faded. 'Listen to me.' He leaned forward in a conspiratory manner. 'I understand you know a man who can introduce inventors to the right people. Is that true?'

'Yeah. Yes. There's a guy comes in here on a fairly regularly basis who claims to have all the right connections. He calls himself The Silver Fox.'

Sergei picked up a beer mat, folded in two, and then reversed the fold. He reversed it twice more and created two semi-circular halves. He selected a pen from the several suspended on a strip of white plastic lining his shirt pocket and wrote a telephone number on one of the halves. 'Would you be so kind as to give him my telephone number?'

'Sure. Any particular time he should call you?'

'No. I'm in and out all the time. Ask him to keep trying if he doesn't get me on his first attempt.'

'Will do. Are you having another pint?'

'Not this time, thank you. I will see you again.'

'Listen. My name is Dave.' He stretched out his hand toward the man on the other side of the bar. 'You?'

'Sergei. Sergei Rabinovitz.' He shook Dave's hand.

'Well, Sergei, I can give The Silver Fox your number and ask him to call you, but I can't vouch for his honesty. Make sure you protect your interests.'

Sergei smiled once more. 'That I will do, my friend. Thank you.'

~

The next day, Dave gave Brian Carter the half beer mat on which Sergei had written his telephone number.

'What's he got?' The Silver Fox wanted to know.

'No idea. The guy just asked if I knew you.'

'What's he look like?'

'I dunno. Russian, Eastern European, something like that.'

'Could he be another Einstein?'

'I don't think so. He drinks Guinness.'

'What the hell does that signify?'

'No idea, but I'll bet Einstein didn't drink Guinness.'

'Whatever. Listen, I owe you twenty quid. Don't let me forget. Here's another card. Keep it on you and if something like this happens again, you can give them my number. Okay?'

'I thought it was a minimum of twenty pounds.'

'What?'

'You originally told me you would give me a *minimum* of twenty pounds for any contacts I made for you. What's this one going to be worth?'

'How can I know that? If I do make a few coppers on the deal, I'll see you straight. Don't fret over it.'

'I just want to know where my main interests are here. I'm not about to push people into your arms unless it's worth it. Twenty quid is no more than a good tip. Why should I risk losing a good tipper for a one-time payment of twenty pounds?'

'So this guy's a good tipper?'

'I didn't say that.'

'What are you saying?'

'I thought I made that clear.'

'Look, I don't know how much, if anything, I'm going to make on this deal. Rest assured that if I do well out of it, I'll see you right. Okay?'

'Fair enough.' Dave nodded his head and put the man's card into his wallet.

~

Dave saw Bryan in the pub two or three times during the following week but there was no mention of Sergei, let alone the finder's fee. Perhaps it hadn't worked out.

~

One week later, at exactly the same time of day, Sergei entered the pub and ordered a pint that he again sipped at the bar.

'Bryan Carter call you, then?' Dave asked the man.

'No. Nothing. I came in to see if you had given my number to the gentleman.'

'Hell, yeah. Gave him your number the day after you left it with me. He said he would call you. Wanted to know if you were another Einstein.'

'I am hardly that.' Sergei smiled. 'But I have invented a device which will allow anyone to extract the last drop of fluid from any kind of container.'

'Really.' Dave was unable to look impressed.

Sergei's smile broadened. 'Most containers that put out a liquid or a spray, have inside them a tube that does not quite reach the bottom of the container, even aerosols. The manufacturers worry that allowing a tube to reach the bottom could lead to a blockage. Even those canisters that people fill themselves, like weed-killer or soda-water, have liquid left over that people usually throw away. My invention will allow them to use all of the product.'

'Listen,' Dave interjected as he pulled the diary out of his pants' back pocket, 'I've got the guy's number. Here.' He handed Carter's business card to Sergei. 'Why don't you try calling him?'

'Thank you my friend. I will do that.'

The inventor purposefully wrote Carter's name and number in a well-used notebook that he took from his shirt pocket. Once done, he handed the business card back to Dave.

Two days later, Sergei was back.

'You speak to The Silver Fox?' Dave asked as he pulled the man his pint.

'Yes. It seems he had been trying to contact me and I must suppose I was working somewhere else in the building whenever he called.'

'Well, the important thing is that you two have now spoken. What happens next?'

'Ah. Yes. Mr. Carter has someone from Amalgamated Resources Specialist Engineering Systems…I think that's the name…visiting his summer house next weekend and he wants me to go there for a meeting.'

'That's a hell of a mouthful.' Sergei smiled. 'Well…' Dave continued, not sure what he should say next to the man. It seemed a little premature to offer congratulations. 'That's great. I wish you all the luck in the world.'

'Thank you, but I have a favour to ask of you.'

'What's that, then?'

'I want you to come with me.'

The request caught Dave by surprise. 'What? Why?'

'I do not know this man or anybody else at the summer house. I am a very nervous man and I would like someone with me to help me with any language difficulties I might have. Also someone I know to prevent me from feeling isolated.'

'You hardly know *me*! Plus you don't seem very nervous and you speak better English than I do.'

'I am not nervous here in the pub, no. But in a strange place with strange people, where I might have to negotiate with someone, I will find it very tense and that is when my command of the language sometimes leaves me. I would just like to have someone by my side.'

'Will you pay my expenses?'

'Of course. You should not have to ask such a thing.'

'Well, I'll tell you what, Sergei, I have Sunday off and if that's what you want, I'll come along with you. You do know, don't you, that Brian Carter is going to charge you ten per cent of anything you make on the deal?'

'Thank you my friend. I am aware of Mr Carter's fee. I will pick you up in a taxi at nine o'clock on Sunday morning and we shall travel by train. Is that acceptable to you?'

'Yeah, sure. How come you don't have anybody else to go with you?'

'When I arrived from Poland, I was alone and without money. I accepted the job in Greene Mansions and the only time I go out is to come here to drink and read the newspaper in peace. The only people I know are you and my tenants. There is an old lady who I shop for sometimes and, also sometimes, walk her little dog. It yaps. Oh, and perhaps the lady behind the counter at the newspaper store on the corner, and Mario in the Italian restaurant where I like to eat, and other such people. But I have no family or special friends, no.'

'You've got to get a life, Sergei.'

'Maybe now I will. Yes?'

'Let's hope so.' Dave wrote his address on a separate piece of paper and handed it to the inventor. 'See you Sunday.'

~

The Silver Fox met them at the station in bright blue Beemer and Dave asked if he was a City fan. He wasn't. When they got to the house, he made introductions and then excused himself, as he had to prepare dinner. Dave went with him to see what needed doing at eleven-fifteen in the morning for a dinner probably scheduled for around five or so. Sergei joined them both in the kitchen where a dozen thick slabs of steak rested on the large butcher-block table. Bryan took an iron mallet and beat the meat into submission. He then took a dozen, large egg-shaped terra-cotta dishes from a cupboard, separated the tops from the bottoms, and laid both halves on a central kitchen table. Someone had already torn sheets of newspaper into strips to line each dish. Brian poured two or three millimetres of salt over the newspaper in the bottom half of the dish and laid a steak on the salt. Then he reversed the process. Salt, newspaper and the top halves of the dishes cocooned the steaks. Dave and Sergei helped prepare the remaining steaks and the men carried the oval dishes to the garden where red and grey embers smouldered in an open pit. Brian strategically placed the small ovens in the pit and then the three of them used the long dead soil obviously removed when the pit was originally created to cover the ceramic ovals and smouldering embers.

The chef slapped his hands together to rid them of the dirt. 'They should be ready in a few hours. Now, who wants a drink? I have some nibbles too. The local bakery makes up a basketful for us every weekend. You should try some; you'll find they're really good.'

~

At one-thirty, Dave sat down at a table with Sergei, Bryan and an American man named Charles Zuckerman who was interested in hearing about the invention. Sergei offered Zuckerman a proto-type of his invention.

'Did you bring the drawings, et cetera?' Zuckerman asked.

'Yes, sir.' Sergei blushed as he fished in his briefcase.

'Has the thing been patented yet?' Zuckerman asked.

'I sent the papers to the Patents Office about five or six weeks ago, but I understand it can take three or four months before one actually receives the patent.'

'You gotta numbered receipt from them?'

'Yes.'

'Good. That's all you need worry about. Okay, now let's look at what we have here.'

Silence reigned as the man from Amalgamated Resources Specialist Engineering Systems inspected the container and then looked over the drawings. Someone stopped at the table to ask if anyone needed another drink. A breeze blew and Zuckerman had to move quickly to prevent a piece of paper from becoming airborne.

'I'll tell you what,' he said. 'Let me take all this into the bedroom where I can study everything in peace and quiet. Kind of like you going to the pub, eh Sergei?'

'You think I go to the public house for peace and quiet?' Sergei sounded shocked. 'I go to take a drink and to walk in the fresh air.'

'Yeah, whatever. I make it my business to know as much as possible about the people I might be doing business with. Hope you don't mind.'

'No. I have nothing to hide, but your information is not quite correct.'

The American ignored Sergei's comments. 'Good man. See you in an hour or so.'

~

Two residents suggested an afternoon walk and Dave thought it a good to get out of the house and give Sergei an opportunity to relax. Neither of the strangers knew the American, so Dave could not glean any information for Sergei to use. After a while they came to a small, thatched, country pub that claimed to serve the best ales in the county and so three of ramblers decided to put the claim to the test. Sergei stuck to his preferred dark stout. After finishing his pint, Dave congratulated the licensee on his ale.

They arrived back at the house just as Bryan was unearthing the brown eggs. The dinner table was already set. Two open bottles of wine, several unopened bottles and two large wooden bowls containing green salads stood at its centre. Two baskets of warm dinner rolls and a couple of metal dishes on which sat oblongs of yellow butter sat next to the largest pepper mill Dave had seen outside a restaurant. Salt lay in an open dish; a small spoon almost buried beneath its surface. As each dish came out of the pit, the top was removed, the bottom inverted, and a white oval fell onto each diner's waiting plate. Brian demonstrated how to use the heel of a knife to crack open the salt shells and reveal the juicy steaks.

~

After the meal was over and the dishes cleared away, Zuckerman turned to business. 'You must want to know what I think about your invention.'

'Yes. I was getting a little, what do you say, apprehensive.'

'Okay. Here it is. Your idea works. I propose to give you five thousand dollars here and now for your invention. I will give you a further five thousand when you sign over the patent to me. What do you say?'

'I was hoping also to get some kind of payment each time my invention is incorporated into any container that you sell.' Dave was surprised to hear Sergei use the word 'incorporated'.

'That'd be nice, but to tell you the truth we don't intend to use your invention. It'd cost us a fortune. We like it every time the consumer throws away some of the product. He pays for it and he doesn't mind throwing it away. It's a great system.'

Sergei turned ashen. 'You wish to pay me ten thousand pounds just so you can file my invention away somewhere where it will never be found?'

'Dollars. That's it. You got it.'

Everyone at the table watched the inventor wrestle within himself. The silence stretched to discomfort. 'You want time to think it over, Sergei?' Dave asked his ward.

'No thinking it over,' Zuckerman insisted. 'The deal's on the table as of this moment. Five minutes from now, it'll be withdrawn.'

'Hold *on*.' Dave protested.

Zuckerman shot a stern look in Dave's direction. 'You hold on my friend. I've given Sergei here an offer for his invention. It is his to take or leave. I see nothing wrong in that.'

Sergei put his hand on Dave's forearm. 'It is okay. I will take the offer. You can have my invention for ten thousand pounds, sir.'

'I said dollars, not pounds. Ten thousand folding green ones.'

'I know what you said, but I am saying pounds. Ten thousand pounds.' Sergei was perfectly calm and it was plain he had set his mind on the figure.

'That's more than half as much again. And for a product that I'm not about to use!' The American stared at Sergei for about five seconds, possibly looking for a lack of resolve that he didn't find. 'What the hell. Ten thousand pounds it is. You Limeys drive a hard bargain Sergei.'

'Actually, Mr. Zuckerman, I am Polish.'

'Polish, English, it's all the same in love and war my friend.'

Metal chair-legs scraped on the tiled floor as everyone followed Sergei's lead and stood up. He reached across the table and offered his hand to Zuckerman. 'I can't say that it has been a pleasure to do business with you Mr. Zuckerman, but I am glad to have concluded this deal.'

'You come up with any other ideas, you make sure to call me first. You understand.' Zuckerman proffered his business card.

'I'll keep in touch with him, Charles,' said Brian, presumably thinking of his ten per cent. 'Are we all done, then?' He looked at Sergei and the American and, as they both said nothing, he closed the proceedings. 'Fair enough. It's been a good day for all concerned. Drinks?'

~

In the train, Dave asked Sergei if he was happy with the way things had gone.

'I do see the man's logic. However, I am going to pour all my energies into inventing something that will make Mr Charles Zuckerman take a positive stance. Next time, he will pay me much more.'

'Good for you. What do you have in mind?'

'I don't know yet, but it will be something which I trust will be of great benefit to Mr Zuckerman's consumers.'

'And what are you going to do with this money?'

'I will add it to my savings and perhaps, one day, I'll buy another block of flats like Greene Mansions.'

That was the second time the man had surprised Dave. 'You own Greene Mansions?'

'Yes. When the previous owner died, he directed in his will that the property be sold to me at a specific price. It was a very generous gesture, but as he had no close relatives and I had worked for him for so many years, he wanted me to have the property. He gave everything else to charity. I was very lucky.'

Dave pondered Bryan's business card. He saw no need to keep it. After all, the two men saw each other across the bar two or three times a week and on half of those occasions they conversed about events of mutual interest. On the other hand, Brian might one-day move and so it would be useful to have his e-mail address. Plus the man had given him a hundred pounds for making the initial introduction. He wondered what Brian had made from the American…another ten per cent? Who had paid for the food and drink? No matter. The five hundred pounds Sergei had given him had made the experience a pleasant one. Better to keep the card.

Sergei still frequented the pub, but there had been no word of a new invention or a new acquisition of property.

Harry

Dave went to his home town for the funeral of a school chum and decided to go to an old watering hole while he was in the vicinity. It wasn't likely he'd run into any friends from younger days, but it was worth a short taxi ride. There weren't many people in the pub but Harry sat at the bar. It took Dave a couple of seconds to accept it was him; his appearance had changed a lot and Dave wasn't sure he wanted to acknowledge the man. Perhaps the trip down memory lane hadn't been a good idea.

There had been days when he'd wondered if Harry might kill someone. The man used to be involved in at least one fight a week, especially after the pubs closed. That could no longer be the case. Harry's swollen knuckles looked painful and Dave doubted he could straighten his hook-like fingers. He watched him fumble a homemade cigarette out of an old and battered tin box that lay on the bar and nearly offered to help, but realized in time that his recognition of Harry's problem could cause embarrassment. The thought of witnessing the struggle to light the tar-stick made him consider walking through the room to the toilet, but the barman saved the situation by fishing a lighter out of his waistcoat pocket and offering a flame to Harry. The man who was once Dave's friend jerkily placed the cigarette between his lips, sucked air through it and gratefully took the resultant smoke deep into his lungs. He exhaled the used smoke from both his mouth and nostrils, partially obscuring his features for a second or two. Dave realised Harry wouldn't bother handling the cigarette again until he needed to remove the finished butt from his lips. He coughed violently but the cigarette stood its ground.

Despite the anchored roll of tobacco, Dave assumed Harry could talk. He shelved his shame at having thought of walking past his former friend and sat on a stool next to him. He decided to forego the usual banter of folks long absent from each other's lives. 'Do you still watch City?'

Harry turned and instantly recognised Dave. 'Nah,' he said, he too not bothering with the 'it's been a while', or, 'fancy seeing you'. Not that he'd use a word like 'fancy'. His voice had a timbre that only cigarettes and alcohol can give a man, 'It's gotten so expensive these days, I 'ave to content mesell wid seeing 'em on't telly or readin' about 'em in't paper.' The words seemed to catch on something and he coughed again to clear his throat. His eyes looked dull; the fire that had once been there was long gone.

Football had been Harry's life. As teenagers, the pair played together for a suburban team until a developer who needed land on which to build a close of houses purchased the pitch. Harry had been the leading scorer and captain of the team. He was big even then and would bundle defences over like skittles as he headed directly toward their goal. It seemed he scored two or three goals every game, but Dave admitted his memory might be flawed.

Professional scouts often watched the team play but everyone knew who they came to see. Harry could probably have made it to the big show, had he kept a rein on his temper. Unfortunately, every time their defence allowed the opposition to score, Harry would become incandescent with rage. 'What's the point of me bangin' 'em in at t'other end, if you lot are gonna let 'em in at this end? Yer useless, the lotta ya!'

The day he slapped their twenty-six year-old goalkeeper for failing to stop a penalty shot was the day the scouts turned away for the last time. Harry used his fists on a brick wall that night.

When the team disbanded, Harry headed south to look for another side to bully into shape. Dave's job prevented him from going with him.

'If you're gonna play football, then bloody well play,' Harry shouted. 'There'll always be a job but there won't always be a game.'

Dave stayed.

~

Five years later, Harry was back. A crippling tackle had ended his playing days. 'If I'd bin a bloody pro, they woulda fixed me up good,' he bitterly complained.

A local team needed a coach and Harry offered his services. Dave went to watch the first game. Harry paced the sideline, berating his players for their lack of courage and dedication. Dave had tried to get his attention. 'Ease up, Harry. They're playing the game for fun, not to win the European Cup.'

Harry had turned to Dave. 'They 'ave ta learn.' He swivelled his head to look at the game, and then turned back again. 'Ya gotta give it yer best effort, no matter what level yer playin' at.'

Dave couldn't argue the point and knew Harry would never see a distinction between a bunch of guys playing on an open field and those playing on a manicured pitch in a packed stadium.

In another game, when a crude tackle scythed down Harry's best player, he turned to the opposition coach with anger in his eyes. 'That 'ow ya win, is it? If ya can't beat 'em, break their bleedin' legs.'

The man turned his back and, had it not been for the forceful intervention by his own bench players, Harry would have physically assaulted him.

The bench players could not, or would not, prevent an altercation in another game during which one player completely missed the goal when taking a penalty shot.

'Can't score if yer not on target!' Harry sarcastically shouted across the field.

''E did 'is best,' said a woman who Dave assumed was the player's partner.

'Well, 'is best aint good enough,' Harry shot back.

'Who de 'ell d'ya think *you* are?' the angry woman screamed.

'I'm the coach,' Harry told her. 'When 'e's at 'ome, misses, 'e's yours. When 'e's 'ere, 'e belongs ta me. I won't interfere with your domestic situations and I'll thank ya ta keep yer trap shut when it comes ta football.'

The woman didn't know what to say. Her jaw kept opening and closing, while squeaking sounds came from her throat.

A man stepped forward. 'You can't speak to people like that,' he said.

'I just did,' Harry replied.

'Apologise to her, now,' the frail man insisted.

Harry swept his arm away from his body, hitting the protester in the face and sending him to the ground, blood oozing from his nose.

~

Harry was still on parole when he assaulted a referee. The official disallowed a goal because the scorer was offside and Harry strode aggressively onto the pitch. People stood and gawked as the coach made his way purposefully toward the black-clad man. He grabbed the referee's shoulder and spun him around to argue the call. The man put his whistle to his mouth and blew furiously to attract attention. Harry snatched the object away, simultaneously tearing it from the ribbon around his neck. He threw it to the ground and tried to grind it into the mud. The referee looked about for a policeman but didn't see one. He motioned for his assistants to join him.

'It's no use callin' *them*,' Harry shouted. 'That one flagged me man offside, an' t'other's a faggot. Yer on yer Jack Jones.' Harry snapped his head into the referee's face, splitting his nose wide open.

~

On visiting days, Dave heard how Harry managed the prison team with an iron hand. He wondered how many opposing teams they could face, but kept the thought to himself. The prisoners played the guards on a regular basis and, since Harry took over the team, the prisoners had won every game. He assured Dave the players believed that the loss of certain privileges was more than offset by the pride they felt and the respect of fellow inmates.

~

Dave was running a bar on the Costa Del Sol when Harry was

released from prison. A friend sent a letter telling of Harry's latest problem. The man had somehow become the coach for a team of under-eleven-year-olds. Surprisingly, he was very popular, insisting every player on the roster spent significant time on the pitch during every game. When Harry benched a star player to give time to a child with no discernible skills, the star's father turned ugly. After heated words, the man attacked Harry and received a beating, thereby sending the coach back to prison.

~

His cigarette done, Harry carefully pinched the stub between thumb and forefinger, guiding his apparently numb digits by watching his actions in the mirror behind the array of whiskies, vodkas and rums on the other side of the bar. He saw Dave watching.

'Gotta be careful, else I'll burn a finger or a lip,' he said with a smoky whisper. He tried to drop the hand-rolled cigarette-end into an ashtray, but it stuck to his thumb and he had to use his other hand to knock it loose. 'These 'ands.' He looked down at them, sighed, turned them over and then back. 'They're a bloody chore an' getting' worse alla time.'

~

Both men had always supported Manchester City and Harry had once been convinced he would play for the team. He had knocked on their doors so often; management had been on first name terms with him. Dave was saddened on hearing his friend could no longer afford to see their games.

'How about I get us a couple of tickets for their next home game?' he suggested.

'Nah. Those days're done, thanks. I've got me a woman now and we just go out for a beer now and then. We're 'appy that way. She'll be 'ere soon ta pick me up. Maybe you'll meet 'er.'

Dave thought of the women Harry had known. There hadn't been a feminine one in the bunch. Women didn't work their wiles on Harry; they just recognised a hunger in him that matched their own. They were pub pick-ups, good for a quick lay and nothing else. Nobody needed a name and nobody had a telephone. Dave wondered what the phrase 'got me a woman now' encompassed.

'So, what's her name, then?' he asked.

'Valerie. She's same age as me, used ta be a nurse. She's 'ad the 'ard times, too.' He asked Dave what time it was. 'She'll be 'ere soon.' He was silent for a few seconds. 'It was 'er as found me. It'll never cease to amaze me that someone as good as 'er could see anything worth 'avin' in me. Just goes ta show.'

'How long have you been together?' Dave asked.

'Oh, I dunno, a couple of years now. It's got so I wouldn't know 'ow to do without 'er.' He rubbed the back of a hand under his chin. 'She's the one as shaves me every day. I'd probably cut me own throat if I was ta try an' do it. I offered ta grow a beard but she wouldn't 'ave it. Trouble is, with me 'ands getting' worse, I even 'ave trouble wipin' me arse. I'll top mesell before I let her take over that job.'

Dave didn't know how to react and covered the silence by calling for two more beers. Harry grinned. 'That were a real conversation stopper, wernit? I'll 'ave ta keep that to meself in future, an' I'd be 'appy if you'd do the same.'

~

They were drinking in silence when the barman called out to a customer. ''Ello, Valerie. Will it be the usual, luv?'

Dave pushed his money to the serving side of the bar to tell the man he would pay for the drink and then turned to see Harry's lady. His gaze swept past Harry's face and he noticed the dullness had gone from his eyes. He looked happy.

Dave's initial impression was she was used to more than 'a beer now and then', as Harry had suggested. She had wrinkles on her face and her eyelids were getting heavy. Hair dyed brown reached her shoulders but grey roots showed at a central parting. On the other hand, her lips seemed firm and there was a brightness in her eyes. Large earrings danced beneath stretched lobes as she came to a stop beside Harry. She had an expression of lightness and love that put Dave in mind of an aging angel.

'How's ma man?' she asked.

'Yer man's fine,' Harry answered, and then he waved a crooked hand in Dave's direction. 'This 'ere's, Dave, an old friend of mine. We 'aven't seen each other in a few years. When we was teens just outta school, we both played for a team up Crumpsal way. 'E used ta scamper down't wing and centre the ball fer me ta score.'

Valerie stretched her arm in front of Harry and he rocked backwards to allow them the space in which to shake hands. 'Pleased to meet you, Dave. Was this a chance meeting?'

He shook her hand. 'Likewise. Yeah, I came in for a pit stop and saw Harry here at the bar.'

She nodded. 'It's a wonder you recognised him.' Her eyes smiled over the rim of the glass. 'Thank you.'

'My pleasure. You seem to have made my friend a happy man.'

After another sip of beer, she smiled again. 'We try, don't we, luv?' She picked up Harry's hand and started to raise it. Dave saw his friend wince as he tried to straighten his fingers. Valerie lowered her head so her cheek touched the back of his hand. 'I love him.'

Dave smiled at Valerie and then turned away to pick up his beer as Harry raised the sleeve of his other arm to blot his eyes.

Dave had written Valerie's number on a piece of paper the barman provided. He turned it over, as if to see if there was a note on the back. There wasn't. His instinct was to throw the paper away but then he thought it a callous thing to do. He wondered if things had gotten so bad that Harry had topped himself. He didn't relish the idea of calling Valerie's number to find out how they were, and suffered another rush of guilt. He'd tell Jane about the friendship and the recent encounter and see what she had to say on the matter. He put Valerie's number in the book under Harry's name.

Behind the Curtain

Dave met a woman's eyes as her gaze swept the room. The brief contact had been enough to impel him to grab two glasses from a passing tray and head for the lonely beauty in the low-cut dress.

'You need a refill,' he said to the woman now seemingly engrossed by the dancers.

The brunette cocked her head and turned to look at him with a friendly smile. 'Do I?' She looked at her glass. 'You're right, I do. How sweet of you.'

'I'm Dave. You a friend of the bride?'

'Gerri.' she said. 'Chief bridesmaid, actually. I guess you didn't notice me at the bridal table.'

He almost coloured with embarrassment. 'I did but I somehow didn't put two and two together. Stupid of me. I guess that puts you on the bride's team.'

She let him off the hook. 'It does. So why are you alone?'

'I just broke up with a girl, well, last month. You here with someone?'

'No. I got dumped so el pricko could find someone with regular work hours. It doesn't matter. Being the bridesmaid meant I wasn't short of things to do.'

'Of course.' Dave smiled. 'Well, now the married couple have gone, you'll have less to do. Nice of them to keep the band playing and the drinks flowing. Would you like to dance?'

Gerri gave him her glass to put on a nearby table. When he turned back to her, she opened her arms and he slid a hand around her silk covered hip until it reached the small of her back. The woman glided faultlessly to the music, while Dave concentrated on his steps.

'You dance well,' he said. Lights reflected off her silky hair.

She tilted her head back and her dark-blue eyes shone. 'Thank you. You're not bad yourself.'

He smiled. 'What do you do?'

'I work in the theatre,' she said. 'You?'

'I'm tend bar. Very boring, I'm sad to say. Are you an actor? Should I know you, at all?' He hoped not. The last thing he needed was to put the make on a woman who considered herself a celebrity.

'Heavens, no.' Gerri's laughter was light. 'I work behind the curtain, making sure things run smoothly.'

'What's that make you, an assistant director?'

'More like the assistant to the assistant director, actually.'

'What does that entail?' Dave didn't really care but he needed to get to know the woman whose cleavage mesmerized him.

'Oh, I make sure actors are sober and keeping their hands off each other; that kind of thing. You could say I'm a damage limitation expert.'

'Really? What do you do, drown them in coffee?'

'No, the only cure for drunkenness is time. I try to establish if they're capable of remembering their lines and acting their part without slurring their words, weaving around the stage or, heaven forbid, falling over.'

The lights dimmed and the band started a romantic ballad, and Dave drew Gerri closer. He breathed in her fragrance, smelling and tasting it. She tilted her head slightly and watched his face. She swept the tip of her tongue across her lips and smiled.

Dave's excitement soared and his mind went blank for a second before he realised he had to keep the conversation going. He blinked purposely to regain his focus. 'Do many of them go on stage when they're drunk?'

'A lot more than you'd think. They become tired of playing the same part night after night. It gets them down. Some use drugs, others alcohol. Some have affairs.'

'What happens if they're too wasted to go on?'

'If they're playing the lead there's an understudy, but stars who've earned their way to the top usually don't hit the bottle while they're working. It's generally the big-name rookies who drink, snort and smoke - those who've gained their chance through a television series or by being a famous muso or jock. A lot don't like the discipline of the stage and they long for the imagined ease and mass appeal of the big screen.'

'And the lesser players?'

'They can be a problem, too. Sometimes we reshuffle the cast and cut out a part or the understudy will volunteer to step in, provided he or she is confident they can play the unfamiliar role. And, as I know everyone's lines, I'm sometimes pressed into service as a last resort.'

'Really! How often have you done that?'

'Oh, I don't know…perhaps a dozen times or so.'

The next number had a slightly faster tempo. 'The worst are those who throw up before taking the stage. I've seen actors who've been performing for twenty years get ill before every performance. Someone has to make sure there's a bucket available for them, usually me.' 'Dave involuntarily shortened a step to open some space between them. Gerri laughed at him and closed the space. 'Then they need a breath freshener, especially if they're to kiss another performer. There have been a few leading ladies who've refused to kiss the actor who has lost his pre-show snack.'

The time seemed right. Dave put his hand under Gerri's chin and tilted her face. 'Talking of kissing, I've been wanting to do just that. That all right with you?'

'I was wondering when you'd get round to it.' She put her hand behind his head and pulled his mouth to hers.

The kiss lasted long enough for them to stop dancing. When they disconnected, they smiled at each other before starting to move again. The kiss gave him the confidence to hold her closer but he reluctantly continued the conversation. 'How on earth did you end up with such a job?' Her nose was at his collar and he knew she was smelling him. 'I mean, it seems to me that most people would start out wanting to be an actor. How does one become an assistant to an assistant director?'

Gerri lifted her head and smiled, revealing perfect teeth and he knew he'd been found acceptable. 'You're persistent with this conversation, aren't you? What about you? You said tend bar. Doesn't sound like you make a lot of money, or am I wrong?'

He couldn't help himself. 'I hear things. People get loose lipped when they're imbibing and they let out things meant to be kept private. I've made some good investments based on what I've heard.'

Gerri laughed aloud. 'You make it sound far too easy, Dave.'

He always made it easy for any intended conquest. 'Your job sounds much more interesting. Tell me, why did you become an assistant to a director's assistant?'

'It's where most directors start out. In fifteen to twenty years, you'll see my name in lights. Now, why don't we get a breath of air?' She gave him her most enticing smile; 'I'm getting hot.'

~

Gerri took him to her one-bedroom flat that had two beds at opposite walls. As they undressed in the dark, she drew a heavy, floor-length curtain, cutting the room in two. 'Think of this as your chance to experience what goes on behind the curtain.'

Dave was aghast. 'You mean someone else might be sleeping here tonight?'

'Of course! Would you have my flat-mate sleep on the street?'

'No, not at all. Sorry. I didn't think.'

Gerri kissed the side of his nose. 'Don't worry; I've learned to be a quiet lover.'

'Yeah but…'

'But what?'

He exhaled. 'Nothing.'

~

An hour or so later, they drank orange juice in a kitchen illuminated only by a nightlight.

'When's your flatmate likely to appear?'

'I've no idea. She comes and goes as she pleases. Were you nervous?'

'Not nervous…it's just that…well…her arrival could be a little off-putting, if you know what I mean.'

'Oh, you did all right before. Tell me, what do you feel about investing some of your money in a stage production?'

He stopped his glass on its way to his mouth. 'You don't beat about the bush, do you?'

'I've found it never gets me anywhere. What do you think?'

He screwed up his face. 'It's not something I know anything about.'

'Imagine I'm on the other side of the bar letting slip details of a chance to make a profitable investment.'

He laughed. 'Yeah, that does happen. I'd need to know more.'

'Why not go wild for once in your life. Put twenty-five thousand into our next production. It'll give you a rush to see your money at work and profits can be substantial.'

'Twenty-five thousand!'

'It's only twenty-five. All those things you hear. What's that to you?'

'If it vaporises, it's quite a chunk, actually.'

'It won't vaporise.' Gerri smiled coquettishly. 'Donations to the arts are tax deductable and, besides, a number of seats are always filled, no matter what we put on.'

He laughed. 'I try not to pay too much in taxes so that line won't work. It's not exactly the best come-on I've heard.'

'But if it takes off, there's television, maybe a movie…'

'Which, I'm sure, will attract bigger investors who'll push me to the wings and grab all the major profits for themselves.'

'Well, I was just trying to give you a chance.' Gerri returned the juice bottle to the bottom shelf of the fridge door. The fridge light reflected off the door and, as Gerri's robe gaped open, shone on her exposed breasts. 'If it's not for you…'

Dave swallowed as he looked at the beautiful mounds rising out of the shadows. 'I didn't exactly say that. Oh, what the hell! Yes, I'll pony-up the twenty-five and try to enjoy the ride, subject to checking the liabilities et cetera. Now, can we get back to what we were doing? I want to get as much as possible in before your flatmate arrives.'

'I just love your choice of words, Dave.'

~

Shortly after Michael's return he arrived at the pub.

'How was the honeymoon?' Dave asked.

'Terrific, thanks. What have you been doing while I've been gone . . . other than work?'

'I've been seeing this woman, Gerri. She's a friend of your wife.'

'Yeah, she is. Well, that's great! I like Gerri. She often hides behind her protective curtain but when she draws it aside, there's none better.'

'She seems very committed to the theatre.'

'That she is. Which hat was she wearing when you met her?'

'What do you mean, which hat?'

'Just that. Did she tell you she was an assistant director or an assistant producer? Gerri carries out both duties very effectively. She knows how to squeeze money out of the most reluctant contributors. She tells me she waits until they're vulnerable and then persuades them to invest in her modest productions. So,' Michael continued, 'how much did you cough up?'

Dave remembered the words his ego had eagerly misinterpreted, *you're making this far too easy, Dave*

He had lost almost two thousand, which, considering the enormous risk he'd taken, was almost a relief. He remembered promising himself to be conservative with his money after he'd dabbled in the stock market. He made the same promise to himself again and Gerri's interest in him had waned once he'd recouped less than his investment and declined to go the same route again. He'd been happy to know she wouldn't twist his arm again. He threw her card in the bin.

Forgive us Our Trespasses

Dave smoothed out a small sheet of paper bearing a purple cross at its head. He instantly remembered the face of the woman who had given him the number. He wasn't sure of her name. P-something. Penny? Pat? Pam? Pamela! That was it. She was a nurse's aide and they had joked about Pam the pan lady. The woman had come into the pub one afternoon and asked for an orange juice. She had sipped her drink while inspecting the place, reading signs, notices, and taking inventory of the bottles behind the bar. As the place was quiet she and Dave struck up a conversation. She related to him that she had been a nun but had quit the order. It had taken seven years, but she had eventually realised she could not spend the rest of her life in such an empty existence. Dave had immediately wanted a date with her. The idea of sleeping with a one-time bride of Christ, a woman who had hopefully never had sex in her life, was appealing.

'How long have you been out?'

'Three weeks. I live at a half-way house a couple of blocks from here that's run by a monsignor.'

'What do you want to do that you haven't yet gotten around to?'

'Have a drink in a pub, which is why I'm here. Do you think the wine you sell here is the same one the church uses?'

'I don't know. I guess it depends on how much they want to spend. Probably not, now I think about it. I mean why give people a good wine when they're only taking a sip? Besides there are so many different reds, and would they buy a branded product?' He poured a few drops into a glass and slid it across the bar. 'Here, this is one of our popular ones, see what you think.'

The woman took a sip. 'Oh, this is quite nice; much better than the stuff we had. Sister Amata and I stayed up one night and drank ourselves silly on the communion wine. I had acid indigestion for hours afterwards. We thought we'd get into trouble, but nobody seemed to notice. Talking about things I want to do; I'd love to go to a football match where the crowd sings all their team songs. I've seen it on television and I'd love to be at a game.'

It had not been Dave's hoped-for choice. 'I could arrange that. The language can get a little blue. Will you mind?'

'No, not really. It's something I'll have to get used to, isn't it?'

'I suppose so. I never thought about it 'til now; suddenly being exposed to it. We all grow up learning it gradually, though I suppose I had a foul mouth by the age of nine or ten.' Pam smiled. 'Blackburn Rovers are playing West Ham tomorrow. Shall I get us a couple of tickets?'

'Yes please. That sounds nice. Oh, but I can't pay for the ticket. Sorry.'

'It's my pleasure. I don't know if I'd use the word 'nice'. We can go to a pub I know for a beer and some shrimp before the game. I have to work tomorrow night but I have Sunday free. Would you like to have brunch somewhere and then maybe see a film after that?'

'I'd love to.'

~

Pamela had clapped her hands in delight at the songs sung by both sets of fans. At halftime, some Blackburn fans had taken it upon themselves to teach Pam the words to a couple of their specific chants. 'Chim chimery, chim chimery, chim chim cheroo. We hate those bastards in claret and blue.' Dave had inwardly cringed at the word 'bastard', but Pamela had not cared and she sang the song with enthusiasm.

All she learned of a second song was, 'You're not singing over there.' But when Blackburn scored their second goal and the West Ham fans fell silent, she repeatedly sang the words as loud as she could and pointed a finger at the claret and blue section of the crowd. Later, a West Ham player shot wide of a gaping goal, the crowd chanted, 'you dick, you dick, you dick. Pam joined in. 'you dick, you dick, you dick.' Dave cringed. She turned to him. 'It amazes me how the chanting of a man's name can be used so effectively.'

'It's not his bleedin' name,' a man in front of her said.

'Really? His name isn't Richard?'

'The word's slang for part of a man's body,' Dave told her.

'Part of his body? What part is…? Oh. Oh no. And I've been chanting it. You must never tell anyone. Promise?'

Dave smiled. 'Yeah, I promise.'

Blackburn won the game and, as the pair left the stadium, Pamela applauded the players and waved at the fans. Dave felt sure she would have behaved exactly the same way if West Ham had won the game.

~

The following day they had enjoyed brunch near Hyde Park and, afterwards, as it was such a sunny afternoon, had changed their plans and taken a stroll. When the sun dipped and the temperature dropped, Dave suggested they retire to his apartment for some hot chocolate.

'Is that an invitation for some sex?' Pamela asked with unnerving bluntness.

'It could be. I guess we'll have to see how matters progress.'

'That's another reason I came into the pub – to find someone to have sex with. I would like to have sex with you.' Dave suppressed a cheerful grin. 'My only experience has been with the monsignor who runs the half-way house and he is quite old and usually in need of a bath.'

The cheerful grin died. 'The monsignor!'

'Yes, the man who runs the halfway house. Why are you so shocked?'

'Aren't all priests, nuns and the rest supposed to take a vow of celibacy?'

'That would normally be true but the monsignor has a special dispensation. As he has to prepare women leaving the church for the outside world, he has sex with them all.

'Special dispensation! What a great line.'

'What do you mean?'

'I don't want to upset you Pam, but have you thought this through? A dirty old man is in charge of these naive women and tells them the Pope says he has to screw them in order to make them ready for the outside world. There are people who would kill to get a job like that.' Dave burst into laughter. 'I'm sorry, but in a way, it's hilarious.'

'It's not that good a job. Some of the women are quite a lot older than I am.'

'That depends on how old he is. A fifty year old woman might not look so hot to a twenty year old man, but a sixty-five year old man will see her quite differently.'

'Oh, yes, I suppose you're right.'

'Are you going to report him?'

'I don't know. I don't think so. Nothing can be changed as far as I am concerned.'

'Maybe not, but you've been sexually abused. Don't you want him punished?'

'Not really. It's not as clear to me as it seems to be to you.'

He had taken her hand. 'Come on, it's getting cold. Let's go to my apartment.'

'No, not now. You've given me something to ponder. I have to be alone for a while and think this thing through. There are women who will arrive after me.' She took a notepad and pen out of her handbag. 'Here's my number at the halfway house. Give me a call.'

He had never called her and, as far as he knew, she had never been into the Coach House again. He wasn't sure why, but the thought of her having had sex with the old cleric had served to dampened his ardour. He dropped the paper into the bin.

The Fall

One Tuesday, Ronald Aitcheson, a high flying lunchtime regular handed Dave two tickets for a West End show. The man had to leave town on urgent business and would be unable to attend the performance that night. 'No charge, Dave. As my employer had the nerve to send me away on such short notice, they've already reimbursed me for them. Enjoy.'

'Thanks, Ron,' he'd said with a grin. 'These'll be an open sesame, I hope.' He put the tickets in his pocket and gave the man a double 'on the house'.

~

Dave fancied Jane, an occasional customer, and was always happy to see her walk into the Coach House. If he missed her entrance, he would soon spot her copper-red hair in the bar. When in high-heels, the corporate fitness and health manager's green eyes were about five-feet-eight inches above the ground and looked out from under brown eyebrows.

~

After the lunchtime rush was over, Dave looked up the American corporation where he knew Jane worked. 'Good afternoon. I'm Dave Wilson and I'd like to speak to the manager of your Health and Fitness department.'

'Do you have the person's name?' enquired a superior sounding voice.

'No. Her first name is Jane but I don't know her last name.'

'Is this a personal call?'

'No, it's strictly business.'

'What is the nature of that business?'

'We need Jane to give us some advice on company policy regarding the physical and mental health of our employees.'

'Will that be Banking, International Trading, or Common Holdings business?'

'What?'

'Which department? Banking, International Trade, or Common Holdings?'

'None of them. As I said, I'm calling from outside your company in regard to the physical and mental health of my company employees.'

'It seems to me this is a personal call, something we don't encourage, especially when you don't know the person's last name.'

'Look. Jane has offered to give us free advice in her own time. I'm sorry I don't know her surname, maybe she thought we already knew it. In any case, her generosity is something that will be beneficial for my company's employees and the reputation of the company for which you work. Do you see harm in that?' He didn't wait for a response. 'Now, will you please afford me a little co-operation?'

He heard a dramatic sigh. 'The woman's name is Dobson. If you care to leave your name and number I'll see Ms Dobson gets it.'

Dave gave the woman his details and asked her to stress to Ms Dobson that the matter was urgent.

Half an hour passed and Jane hadn't called. He dialled a second time and, as he now knew Jane's last name, found her extension.

'Dobson.'

'Hello, Jane. This is Dave Wilson … from the Coach House. I have two tickets for 'Cats' tonight and wondered if you'd like to go with me. We could grab a bite afterwards. What do you say?'

'Hi, Dave. Would that be a bite to eat?'

He laughed. 'Yeah, a bite to eat.'

'Actually, I've already seen 'Cats'.' Dave's high plummeted. 'I saw it in New York, but I'd love to see it again.'

His high returned. 'Great. Can we meet in the pub around six thirty or so?'

'Sounds good. See you then.'

'Excellent. Oh, by the way…'

'Yes.'

'You might get a message from some witch I had to deal with because I didn't know your last name. I told her you had offered to assist us with advice on a mental health and fitness policy for company employees. I hope I didn't get you into any kind of trouble.'

'A fitness policy for pub employees?'

'I didn't tell her I worked at a pub. I just gave her the number without explaining further.'

'Don't worry about it. See you six-thirtyish.'

'Good, see you then.'

After he hung up, Dave put the paper on which he'd written her number between the pages of his diary.

His boss was happy to allow him to leave before his shift ended. The 'after work quickie' session would still be busy, and it would be a good time for her to have one of her periodical 'meet the punters' sessions.

He wore the Italian suit and accessories purchased in New York and thought of Kate as he dressed. He was happy as he walked back up the hill to the pub, past Greene Mansions, the Trattoria, and the numerous antique shops to the pub. Jane arrived in a taxi. She wore a simple black Spanish jacket over a low cut dress of the same material and a single strand pearl choker. Dave's boss gave them each a drink and embarrassed them by loudly asking everyone in the bar to agree they made a beautiful couple. It was a relief when the driver of their taxi came into the pub looking for his fare.

~

After the show, the couple walked to a nearby restaurant for dinner. The song, Memories kept going through Dave's head and he tried to sing it. He didn't know many of the words, so he lah-dee-dahed a lot.

'You are a really bad singer!'

'I've been told that, but I've always considered my lack of talent is compensated by my enthusiasm.'

'Disavow yourself of that notion. You're terrible.'

'Really?' He refused to be deflated. 'You should hear me in a shower. I do an excellent impersonation of Gene Kelly Singing in the Rain.'

"How old are you?'

'Oh, come on. You must've seen that film clip on the telly; surely everyone has.'

'Mmm. Are you talking about a shower in your bathroom or out here on the street?'

'On the street of course. There are no lamp-posts in my shower at home.'

'Of course. Silly of me. I would normally take your word for it, but I have to say the sounds in my head aren't flattering.' Her smile was fetching, but Dave knew the time was not yet right to kiss her.

They were shown to a corner table with a white stuccoed wall on one side and a window looking out on the street on the other. The tables around them were full and Dave was glad he had made the reservation. He helped Jane take off her jacket and draped it on the back of her chair. He ordered a bottle of wine before they read the menu.

'Was it as good as the New York production?'

'What? Oh. Yes. I love the show, especially the music.'

'Except when I'm singing it!'

She laughed. 'That's not the music's fault.'

'It could be.' He gave her his best smile. 'I'm glad you enjoyed the show. I've been thinking to get a date with you for a while.'

'Is that what this is, a date? I didn't realise. I thought we were just two acquaintances sharing a social occasion together.'

Dave felt his face flush as he searched for a response, 'I guess I didn't specify I was asking you out on a date. Stupid of me. That kinda leaves a big question-mark in the air, doesn't it?' He lifted his hand and drew the symbol, making a forceful dot with his index finger.

Jane smiled as she reached and pulled Dave's hand down to the table's surface.

He grinned. 'We can still enjoy ourselves, can't we?'

'Hey, a date is fine by me.' Once she had his hand in more accessible territory, she entwined her fingers with his. 'It's just that I didn't prepare for it. Physically or mentally. Just give me time to get my head in the right place and everything will be fine.' Dave squeezed her hand…partially with affection and partially with relief.

'Why haven't you asked me for a date before? I've sat at the bar on several occasions just waiting for you to ask me out.'

His eyebrows rose. 'You've always been with other people.' He was losing control of the conversation. 'I was a little worried that a corporate type would look down on dating a barman. I wanted a situation to which you'd say yes. Asking you out for a drink seemed a bit lame.'

'I'm hardly the corporate type. Anyway, what seemed lame; the drink or the reason?'

'Definitely not the reason.' The woman was fun.

'Women aren't as shy as you seem to think.'

'So why didn't you do the asking then?'

'I don't know. Maybe I'm not as forward as I claim to be. I mean, what would a handsome barman who gets to meet more women in a day than I've have dinners in a month see in a corporate type like me?'

'Touché!' He smiled again. 'I imagine you're in heaven, seeing all those guys in their little shorts and vests all day long.'

Jane laughed. 'No. No. The young hunks go to their own gyms or haven't yet considered working out. I mostly get the older guys who are happily married and have realised it's time to take care of their bodies before they pay the price for not doing so. Them and the women, of course.'

Dave laughed with relief, hoping Jane would think he was laughing at her humour. She smiled back at him and looked so enticing that he rose, pressed his tie to his stomach, leaned across the table and gently kissed her on the corner of her mouth. The positioning of the kiss was open to interpretation and he waited for

Jane's reaction as he pulled back to sit on his chair. He took her left hand as he started to descend. His chair was a little lower than he anticipated and he sat down with a slight jolt. He heard a crack and felt himself falling. As he headed for the floor, he saw Jane's eyes grow wide and her mouth open with alarm. Her right hand joined her left in holding on to Dave, but to no avail. As he hit the carpet his hand slipped from her grasp.

'Are you all right?' she asked with concern as she rushed around the table and bent over to assess any harm.

'I'm fine, thanks.' His humiliation dissipated as he looked down the front of her gaping dress. When his gaze returned to Jane's face, he saw she was aware he had been ogling her breasts. He grinned with embarrassment and got to his feet. Jane brushed his jacket with the serviette she still held, although there was no evidence of dirt. He picked up the chair and saw the back right leg had broken off. 'Bloody chair!'

'Are you sure you're all right?' Jane fussed. 'Take off your jacket and let's see if there's any damage.'

'No. Look, I'm embarrassed enough without stripping off my clothes.'

She raised her eyebrows. 'Really?'

Dave did as instructed and was not happy to see Jane put a hand to her mouth to cover a laugh. 'Your trousers are badly torn, Dave. I do like the lipstick kisses all over your shorts, though.'

'What do you mean torn?' Dave felt his right buttock and realised that a seemingly large flap of material hung down and exposed his boxer shorts. Thankfully, said shorts seemed intact.

A concerned waiter arrived.

'Can you get me a safety pin?' Jane asked him.

Diners at the next table had stopped eating. 'You should sue these people for all you can get,' one of them advised.

'I do like those shorts,' a woman observed. 'Where did you get them?'

'Good form,' said another. 'I'd give it a nine.'

'Shush,' said his companion. 'He might be hurt.'

'I missed it,' said someone at another table. 'Could you do it again?'

Dave wondered if the fiasco might put an end to a relationship not yet begun.

Jane smiled mischievously, put her hand behind his head and pulled it down to a level where she could kiss him on the cheek and whisper in his ear. 'You have to admit there's a funny side to this. It definitely beats Singing in the Rain. If I laugh now, I promise I'll make it up to you later.'

'In that case, feel free to laugh.'

Her eyes sparkled and Dave forgot about his exposed posterior.

The waiter arrived with a safety pin which Jane used to attach the flap of material back to the rest of Dave's trousers.

The manager joined the still hovering waiter. 'Can I take it you're unharmed, sir?' He didn't wait for confirmation. 'Please, stay and enjoy your meal. There will be no charge, naturally.'

'That's great, but what about my suit? It's ruined!'

The manager noticed other diners were showing interest in the situation. 'We will be happy to reimburse you for the cost of a new suit, sir. Please buy one of your choice and bring the receipted invoice to us for payment.'

'Thank you.'

'Not at all, sir. We are only sorry you had such an unpleasant experience. We've been using the chair, all these chairs, for quite some time and never had an occasion like this before. Are you sure you're all right? You haven't suffered any physical damage to your person?'

'No, I don't think so.'

Some diners stood to examine their chairs.

Pierre delivered a replacement chair whilst a second waiter arrived with the first course. The manager took the opportunity to depart. 'Bon appetite!'

'Are you sure you want to stay?' asked Jane.

'It's a free meal so we might as well take advantage.'

~

The realisation that the right trouser leg was now hitched higher than the left caused Dave to affect a limp when they left the restaurant.

The couple took a taxi to Jane's flat where she examined the bruise on Dave's rear-end and pronounced him fit for duty.

~

The following Saturday, they went together to buy Dave a new suit. The lovers, receipt in hand, then set out for the restaurant to obtain reimbursement.

They had to wait a few minutes before the manager appeared. His professional smile quickly turned into the frown of someone clearly less than pleased to see them. 'Good day, sir, madam.' He shot his cuffs as he walked toward them.

'Good afternoon.' Dave was determined to be polite. 'Do you remember me? One of your chairs collapsed under me and tore my suit.'

'I do remember the unfortunate incident, yes Sir.'

'I have the receipt for my new suit. You promised to reimburse me for its cost.'

'A whole suit! I said get new trousers and we would reimburse you for that. Not a whole suit!'

'I beg your pardon? You told me to get a new suit. Besides, where the hell,' Jane nudged him to remind him to keep his cool, 'am I going to find trousers made from the exact same material as the jacket? I got the original suit in New York, for Christ sake.' Jane nudged him again.

'All right, all right. There's no reason to raise your voice. Let me see the bill.'

Dave handed over the receipt.

'You can see Mr. Wilson didn't buy the most expensive suit he could find,' Jane said. 'He's been fair with you and you should be fair with him. You should also reimburse him for the cost of taking a taxi. He could hardly have taken the underground.'

The manager looked at Jane over the top of his half-moon bifocals. 'You have a point.' He paused and licked his lips. 'The owner is not here presently. Perhaps you could return next Tuesday or Wednesday and we'll finalise the affair. He is only here during the day, so please arrive before four o'clock.'

~

Dave worked eleven to seven on Tuesday and was unable to go to the restaurant. He called the manager. 'Hi, this is Dave Wilson.' The man did not respond. 'I tore my suit on one of your chairs.'

'Ah yes, Mr. Wilson. How are you today?'

'I'm fine. Have you had a chance to speak to the owner yet regarding reimbursement for my suit?'

'Not yet. I expect him to be here sometime this afternoon and we can hopefully clear this up tomorrow. Will you stop by?' Was the man looking for a negative response?

'I'll be there around one o'clock.'

~

The following afternoon, the manager apologised for the owner's absence but paid Dave in cash for the full amount of the receipt, plus an additional ten pounds to cover the taxi fare. There were no apologies, nor any attempt to convince him to dine in the place again.

He called Jane. 'They paid up in full and in cash,' he told her.

'So, all's well that ends well?'

'I guess so.'

'You guess so? Let me tell you something. When you told me we were on a date, you surprised me. I mean I was happy that it was a date, but there was no way we were going to sleep together that night.'

'But we did sleep together.'

'That's right. Do you know why?'

'Because I fell off the chair?' Dave ventured.

'Not exactly. Why don't you think about it and tonight we'll see if you've figured it out.'

Jane told him he was waffling when he tried to come up with the reason she slept with him on their first date. His best line, 'what reason was there not to?' had been snorted at. She never had explained it, and Dave wondered if it could have been a reward for not starting Singin' in the Rain. He stared at the paper on which he had first jotted Jane's work number. That, plus her mobile and home numbers, were all committed to memory, but he decided to enter them into his new diary as the thought of not doing so felt wrong. Once done, he dropped the balled betting slip into the bin.

Kiss Me Hardy

The majority of the pub's pre-lunch clients had had their croissants and cups of freshly brewed coffee. Some read newspapers attached to reading sticks kept near the fireplace. Others downed their early 'fixes' and scanned the racing pages. Dave was in the men's toilet, pinning the sports pages to the wall above the urinal. The courtesy ensured that imbibers making room for more of the good stuff had something to do other than whistle and inspect their non-liquid assets.

There was no roar of machines to announce the arrival of the black-clad crowd. They entered the pub in groups of two, three or four. They were quiet and well behaved, but his co-worker, Ellen, maintained that was only because they were sober.

'There'll be trouble if they stay 'ere for long,' she said.

As the crowd grew and it became clear the men meant to stay a while, Dave wondered about Ellen's scenario.

'Take care of things for a moment. I'm going to ask the boss to bring Jack in to help us behind the bar, maybe a couple of bouncers as well.'

A man for whom Ellen poured a drink overheard his words. 'No need for bouncers, we have our own. We realise we're perceived as a threat. That's why we police ourselves and do our utmost to prevent problems from occurring. You'll see guys wearing ID cards. They're our marshals and they'll put a stop to trouble before it begins. You shouldn't notice a thing. If there is a problem needs sorting, let me know.' The man grasped the card that dangled from his neck, looked at it and then turned it around for both Ellen and Dave to see. 'Hardy's the name, and I'm in overall charge of this bunch.'

Dave still went to see his boss. When he entered the woman's office, he found she had already called Jack in, as well as waitresses and extra kitchen staff.

~

'Where are your bikes, then?' Dave asked one man as he served him a pint of Guinness.

'Down by the park.'

'Hyde Park?'

'Yeah. We hired a parking lot for the weekend. That way, we don't have to drink and drive.' The man grinned. 'We maintain our image by travelling on the underground and scaring the commuters.'

Dave smiled at the image. 'So why do some of you still carry your helmets?'

The man shrugged his shoulders. 'For some guys it's a badge; others worry about theft.'

'Not because it's some sort of status symbol then?'

The man wiggled his head from side to side, as if weighing the question. 'Status symbol, or badge. Does it matter?'

'Not at all. I'm just chatting. Is this a special occasion?'

'Sort of. We come from all over the country and on six or eight weekends a year we meet up somewhere. This time, it's West London. Someone in the group had been to this place previously and recommended we honour you with our company.'

Within an hour, there were almost a hundred bikers in the pub. Many had seemingly dallied at the numerous antique shops encountered on the walk up the hill from the tube station to the pub. A few had purchased small items and were re-examining them or showing them to friends. There was talk of costly purchases and bargains made.

~

The regular customers had silently returned the newspapers to their appointed location, finished their coffees and disappeared; some to the betting shop across the road.

Only 'Old Tom' remained in his usual seat at the table in the far right-hand corner of the public bar. The man had been around longer than the staff. He wore an old overcoat over a wrinkled pair of trousers and a white collar-less shirt that had turned grey over the years. He always had a week's growth of white beard. His 'cheese-cutter' cap never left his head. Tom did not believe in paying for his drinks and it was a rare day when he bought one for someone else. He sat at the dominoes table on a small, L-shaped bench at the junction of two walls. When he wasn't playing, he turned the tiles face down and waited for his next opponent. The stake was always a drink. The man rarely lost and so he spent most of his day at the table, only rising to visit the bathroom. Many regulars played a quick game of dominoes on their arrival at the pub. Some were interested only in allowing the old man to believe he had earned his pint of best bitter. Others tried to win and they sometimes succeeded, but many of them still insisted they buy the loser a pint. Young men calling in for two or three drinks before meeting their girlfriends or 'going up West' for the night greeted him warmly and often played a fruitless game to amuse the old man. They would tell him about their successes with the opposite sex and Old Tom would smile. The bikers took to Tom as if the Coach House was their local. Men stood and watched as the old man dispatched one after another of their tribe. He had never had so many willing punters and the pints added to his tab behind the bar would last him for at least a week.

~

Men in black T-shirts and leather vests scanned the white and pink business pages and the stock prices. Others, some of whom were wearing black German Infantry helmets, flicked through the pages of *Time* and *Newsweek*. Snatches of overheard conversations on mobile telephones revealed some of the men were doctors and lawyers. A film and television actor who had played innumerable small parts was instantly recognisable, but whose name no staff could recall.

Dave was at first surprised by what he witnessed, but as he surveyed the pub he was thankful he was not serving drinks to a chapter of the Hell's Angels or Crypts Motor Cycle Gangs. Although some of the men were large and well-muscled, they did not have the hard veneer expected of bikers. There were a few tattoos in view, but most men displayed clean skin. Some sported pirate-like earrings, but the majority of bodies looked un-pierced. The clothing was common to all, but it was the clothing of motorbike riders, not the uniform of gang members. A lot of jackets bore advertisements for Harley Davidson motorbikes. Other bikes advertised were, Norton, Nightwing, Thundercat, Zephyr, Superdream and Agusta Strada F4.

~

The drinks flowed and the kitchen was busy. Beer and scotch were very popular but so were sherry and gin. Steaks and curries vied with salads and omelettes.

A man with diamond studs in his lobes asked Dave, 'All right if we play our boom-box?'

The pub didn't have a jukebox and all the regulars except 'Old Tom' were long gone. 'Sure,' Dave told him. 'But I need you to keep the volume at an acceptable level.'

He continued to read the different motifs on the clothing as he served drinks. 'Oh, Bugger me!' seemed strange. 'Joy Ride 'didn't fit in with black clad bikers. Neither the moustachioed men holding hands nor the two men kissing in the corner fit Dave's image of gang members.

He turned to Ellen. 'These guys are gay.'

'Well, aren't you the fast one on the uptake, then!'

'I knew some of them were, but it's taken me till now to realise the whole bunch are.'

The music of Barbra Streisand, Judy Garland and Peter Allen filled the air. Everyone sang, '*I Go to Rio*' and '*Just a gigolo*'. '*Bi-coastal*' received a lot of vocal support.

The travelling bouncers quickly quelled a small commotion at the back of the room. One of them came to the bar, 'Nothing to worry about. One of us wanted to physically display his love for another, but we nipped it in the bud – so to speak.'

Change returned after drinks or food were purchased, was often deposited in a box that appealed for funds for the training of guide dogs.

'They could always give me a tip, if they want to get rid of their money,' Ellen said under her breath.

~

Some of the pub regulars stepped through the door during the afternoon but once they saw the mass of black-clad men, they discretely withdrew. One customer, who the staff dubbed, 'The General' because of his clipped accent and military style, appeared at the door twice in one hour. He usually arrived around six on weekday evenings and sipped two gin-and-tonics as he read the Evening Standard. He always wore a three-piece, charcoal grey suit and a Welsh Guards tie. The third time he opened the door, he entered the pub and strode to the bar with a brown paper bag containing whatever purchases he must have just made. He was dressed in a tweed sports jacket with patches at the elbows, a white open-necked shirt and a yellow cravat with riding crops on it.

'Howdyado. Usual please.'

Dave made the man his drink. 'Not often we see you in here at the weekend.'

'No. Had some shopping to do and then walked around the neighbourhood for a while. Lovely day. Thought I'd treat meself to a gee and tee. Unusual crowd you've got. Like this every Saturday?'

'No. I understand we've been recommended.

'Um' the man sipped his drink. 'Must always be prepared. Scouts motto and one of life's rules, what!'

~

The temperature in the crowded pub became uncomfortable so Dave opened the door to the street and fixed it in place with a wedge. The air-conditioning system had never been intended for such a large crowd. The bikers discarded jackets and vests. Dark patches of perspiration framed in white appeared on the black T-shirts. The stripping revealed more interesting lettering:

'Yukazegaze'

'Warning: hot exhaust pipe!'

'Salt Peter'

'Backfiring strictly prohibited'

'Ramrod'

'Lesbefriends'

'Tube steak'

'My other phallic symbol is a scooter'

Men stood with arms around each other's waists and shoulders. One man stripped the tee shirt off his companion's back but when Ellen told the wearer to put it back on, he did so.

~

When two policemen walked through the door, the noise level dropped and all eyes settled on the uniformed lawmen.

'Do you know you have customers drinking outside?' the sergeant asked Dave.

'No, I didn't. Thanks for telling me.' Dave hurried to the gate at the end of the bar. 'I'll bring 'em back in straight away.'

'Yes. I think the expression right away might be more appropriate. Bringing 'em inside would probably be a good idea, seeing as 'ow you only 'ave a licence for alcohol to be consumed *on* the premises.'

'I'll take care of it, Sergeant.' Dave grabbed one of the bouncers, 'You've got to keep everybody inside the pub or we'll all be in trouble.'

'No problem, consider it done.' The man bounded out to the street. 'Right, everyone back inside,' he shouted. There were a few sounds of protest. 'It's not a request, it's the law.'

The violators made their way back inside and the two policemen seemed content.

'Keep your eye on the situation.'

'Will do. Thanks.' Dave told the lawmen.

As the two men stepped out of the door and on to the sidewalk, the bikers cheered, whistled, and banged their glasses on the tables. The General, who had removed his jacket, grinned boyishly. The policemen checked their step, and then continued on their way.

~

Some of the men took to sitting on low stools that surrounded bar tables and were thereby unable to place their arms around waists or over shoulders. Consequently, some slipped their non-drinking arm around their partner's leg and underneath their crotch. The standing men shifted their stances to facilitate the fondling of genitals. Bouncers quietly moved amongst the group and reminded them they were in a public place.

~

By late afternoon, The General had consumed half-a-dozen drinks. He left his place at the bar and mingled with the bikers, stopping to talk with two or three, before moving to a new group. After the first two drinks he had changed the gin measure to 'a double'. He had removed his cravat, but his white shirt and cavalry twill pants marked him.

A lone man sat in the far-left corner of the room, head lowered, tears running down his nose and into his glass of scotch. Another man went over and put his arm around the heaving back.

Two men arm-wrestled across a table, while others looked on, cheered, and called for a match against the winner. The domino games continued.

The General returned to the bar and ordered another, 'large gee and tee, if you will, old boy.'

~

Couples began to depart; some hand in hand, others with arms around another's shoulders.

Hardy went to the bar to talk with Dave. 'We're leaving now, albeit in dribs and drabs. We've cleaned the toilets as best we could with what was available. If, after we've gone, you find any damage, or find the carpet needs cleaning, please get in touch with me.' The man handed Dave three business cards. 'We like to leave on good terms. You've done us proud with the service and food. I know we took over the establishment and we all thank you for being so hospitable. Maybe we'll see you again.'

'It'd be a pleasure,' Dave told the man, 'but next time, do us a favour and call in advance.'

'Yes, I know. It was our intention to contact you this time, but our co-ordinator, Maurice, suddenly had to go overseas on a business trip and he neglected to tell us he hadn't called you. We anticipate encountering the same problem elsewhere.'

Two of the bouncers joined their leader at the bar. 'Are we

allowed to have a drink now?' one of them asked the headman.

'Provided the other bouncers are keeping off the stuff, yes.'

'Two very large pints of your best bitter please,' the second man demanded with a broad smile. Dave put down the business cards and pulled the drinks.

'It's gone well,' the second bouncer said, turning to Hardy.

'Thanks in part to you two. You should remove your identity labels now.'

The General picked up one of the business cards and read the details.

Hardy continued. 'What about those going to the theatre? Can we account for them?'

'Pretty much. Those who left said they were going back to their hotels. If we get everybody still here to leave within the next fifteen minutes, they'll be okay.'

'Robert Hardy?' The General asked.

'Yes, that's me,' the group leader responded as he turned and faced The General.

'Simon Hargreaves. I was the London liaison on that case against the Pakistani government our companies handled last year.'

A smile grew on Hardy's face. 'Simon. So good to meet you after all this time.'

The two men shook hands.

'What are you going to see?' Dave asked as he put the two pints on the bar.

'Swan Lake,' one of the bouncers replied. 'It's a new production of the ballet but with an all-male troupe.'

'Emphasis on butt,' laughed his friend.

The man laughed with him. 'True, however (see how I avoided your but), we're not all going; couldn't get enough tickets. Those without are going to tour the flesh spots in the West End.'

Both men grinned at each other.

~

Hardy and Hargreaves were in deep conversation. Dave started to clean up the bar.

'You didn't mention you were gay,' Dave heard The General accuse Hardy.

'It's not something I announce to people I haven't met. Besides, I don't recall you being forthcoming with the same information.' Hardy grinned.

'Yes, quite right; same position. It's just surprising to bump into you and find you're of the same persuasion. Makes it doubly pleasing for me.' Dave closed his eyes momentarily and shook his head in shock at The General's statement.

Hardy smiled. 'Small world, isn't it?'

'It surely is. There's something I must ask you. Silly really, but I can't let the opportunity go by.'

'What might that be?'

The General put his arm around the man's shoulder, 'Kiss me, Hardy.'

'It's not an original line, Simon, but what the hell.'

Dave lifted The General's drink to wipe the surface of the bar as the two men kissed in front of him. Uncomfortable, he put down the drink, dropped the cloth and turned to gather his composure while he straightened bottles on the back wall of the bar.

~

The last dozen or so men departed together. Jack and Dave left their places behind the bar and helped others clean the pub. They emptied ashtrays, disposed of wet or torn beer mats, put the furniture back where it belonged, straightened the curtains and picked up the multitude of empty and partially empty glasses left on every surface. They wiped down the tables and seats. Jack went for the vacuum cleaner. Ellen washed tray after tray of dirty glassware. They picked food from the floor and returned plates to the kitchen. After three-quarters of an hour, the place was back to reasonable order. 'Old Tom' snoozed in his corner with four untouched pints amid his dominoes.

'Now, all we need is for our regular customers to discover the bikers have gone,' Ellen observed.

'Hey, it's Saturday night. In any case, we *would* be quiet at this time. They'll start coming in around eight or so. You'll see.'

'Not me,' she replied. 'I'm out of here. Two shifts are enough for me.'

Dave remembered he had worked fourteen hours that day. He looked at Hardy's business card. The man worked for a law firm in Birmingham. He had given one of the cards to his boss, but there had been no reason for her to call the biker. Dave crumpled the card and tossed it into the wastebasket. The General had returned to his normal routine without a word to anyone.

Exchange Mart

'Do we like Clapton?' asked Jane.

'What's with the 'we' shit?' Dave responded.

'I'm not sure who he is. Anyway, Sally at work, you don't know her, had two tickets to see him on Saturday but as she'll be in New York she gave them to me.'

'It's Eric Clapton. How much?'

'Nothing. They were a gift from friends throwing a party tomorrow night. All we have to do is attend the party. You want to go?'

~

Mart and Gina Boscarelli, welcomed Jane, Dave and Sally warmly and for fifteen minutes the five indulged in getting-to-know-you talk.

'Martin but everyone calls me Mart. I understand you work at a pub.'

'Yeah, the Coach House on Kensington High Street. You been there?'

'Shouldn't think so; Gina and I aren't pub people.

To fill the lull in conversation Gina said, 'As Sally has to leave early, I'll get the crepes going. Fillings are on the table.'

'No one else coming?' Dave asked.

'No, it's just us,' Mart said with a grin. 'Hope you don't mind.'

'You first,' said Gina as she placed a crepe on Jane's plate. 'Help yourself to whatever.'

Jane piled fruit and cream on her crepe. Dave settled for sugar and fresh lemon juice. He tasted the first mouthful and recalled the pancakes of his childhood. 'This is good, Gina. Thanks.'

Gina laughed at the number of crepes he consumed. 'Don't overdo it, Dave. You don't want to be too stuffed for later.'

'What comes later, then?' asked Dave.

'You'll see,' she replied with a cheery voice.

~

Sally left at nine-thirty. 'Sorry to rush off but I haven't finished packing yet.'

During their farewells Dave noticed Gina shed a few tears. 'She and Steve, - did you know her boyfriend? - have been such good friends.'

Mart put an arm around her shoulders. 'She'll be back one day.'

'Yeah, but living in America is going to change her, plus the years, and…you know what I mean. It'll never be the same again.'

Mart clapped his hands. 'This is far too heavy.' He beamed at Jane and Dave. 'You guys want more wine, or something stronger?'

'I'll stick with the wine,' Dave said. Jane agreed.

Mart refilled their glasses. 'Look what you've gone and done, Gina; you've put a real dampener on the party. Put some music on and cheer the place up. How long have you two been together?' he asked.

'Oh, not that long,' said Jane. She gave Dave a loving smile and he returned a toothy grin.

He knew the Boscarellis were making polite conversation but Mart's facial expression seemed out of place.

'Being a couple is great,' said Mart. 'Happily experiencing everything that men and women have been doing since Adam and Eve got to know each other.'

'Speaking of getting to know one-another,' said Gina, 'When Mart and I first got together, I was surprised by his need of a night-light in the bedroom.'

Jane's smile was wooden. 'Oh, really?'

'He sometimes wakes up to a panic-attack and needs to immediately register his surroundings. We keep the light on at all times.'

'Let me stretch the subject of bedrooms,' said Mart, 'and ask you a question. As you aren't married, do you date other people?'

'No. We're pretty committed to each other,' Dave said as he reached for Jane's hand.

'How much of a commitment is 'pretty committed'?' Jane demanded.

Gina clapped her hands and laughed. Mart wore a grin.

'I am absolutely committed,' Dave said with a smile.

'There's a world of difference between pretty and absolutely,' said Gina.

'You ever think of finding other partners as a couple?' Mart smiled as he spoke.

Gina's glass paused on its way to her mouth.

Jane and Dave looked at each other. Jane stood. 'Can I use your toilet?'

'Upstairs and to the right,' Gina said.

Dave smiled to himself, seeing Jane was shocked. As she mounted the stairs, Mart spoke again. 'Is that a real bathroom call, Dave, or is she leaving you to answer? Perhaps there are hidden desires bubbling below the surface.'

Dave remembered his grandmother saying one should always be polite to strangers. He wondered if her teaching included people like the Boscarellis. He shifted in his chair. 'I think she probably left because the conversation was making her uncomfortable.'

Mart smiled. 'You never know until you ask, do you?' he persisted 'Maybe the real reason Jane left the room was so we can convince you she has desires she's embarrassed to discuss but which we can air in her absence.'

'We're happy with the way things are.' Dave knew his voice sounded testy but he didn't care.

'You seem to be getting uptight, Dave. There's nothing wrong with talking about sex. It's something we all do, like eating. Would you be shocked if we asked you … what … have you seen the movie, *Tom Jones*? Dave nodded. 'Do you remember the scene where Jones eats asparagus dripping with butter? If you'd eaten asparagus that way with Jane, would you tell us about it?'

'No, I wouldn't.'

'Why not?' Gina asked.

'Because it would be something between us, a private moment made more intimate by keeping it to ourselves.'

'That's a convenient stance, but what would you do if you could have sex with another woman as long as Jane didn't indulge herself with another man?' The smile in Gina's eyes annoyed Dave.

'Decline, probably.' Dave hoped he was being truthful.

'Why?' Mart asked. 'Plenty of men fool around outside their marriage. It's probably the biggest reason for divorce, though I don't know why.'

'We're not married and we've only known each other for short while.' Dave's discomfort increased.

'Oh, so it's a time thing. How long should one wait?' Gina pushed. 'A couple of years after you're married? More?'

'No. This is all bullshit!'

'Why? Because once you think about it, it won't you take long before your thoughts turn to action?'

Dave again shifted in his chair. 'Look, I've had enough of this.'

'I'm not surprised. You never mentioned not wanting to cheat on Jane, just that you didn't want to think about it.'

'That's pure semantics.'

'All right.' Mart moved forward so he was sitting on the edge of his chair. 'Let's change tack. What about raw sex? Slam, bam, thank you maam sex?'

Gina slapped his upper arm. 'Not so fast with the slam, bam.'

Mart held up his hands. 'I was merely saying that sex, as a body function, isn't necessarily intimate and can be openly discussed between adults. Look at us. We're two young, good-looking and fit people who enjoy sex. You two seem likewise inclined so why can't we discuss the possibilities?'

Was that an invitation? He was right in his self-description. Gina, a beautiful, sensual, stunning brunette with … no! The thought made him squirm. He didn't know why the conversation negated her attraction but what they were proposing - might be proposing – embarrassed him. It dawned on him that he was turning down a situation of which he had once idly fantasized. Could Jane have disappeared out of shyness, hoping he would negotiate a wife-swap? No. Of that he was sure. He wished she'd re-appear. They would leave as soon as she returned.

'You've gone quiet on us, Dave. More wine?'

'What? Oh, I, I'm sorry; I was miles away. No thank you.'

'Thinking of the possibilities?'

Jane returned. 'I've been on the stairs, listening to the conversation for a couple of minutes and I think what you've been saying is rubbish. My enjoyment of sex is partially based on intimacy with my partner. I can't agree…'

'Haven't you ever had a one-night-stand?' Gina interrupted.

'Yes, but I usually regretted them. Not that there were many.'

'But isn't it usually lack of planning that causes one-night-stands to be regretfully sordid? On the other hand, animal sex with the right people in the right circumstances can be wonderful.'

'Perhaps,' Jane agreed reluctantly, 'but the circumstances you're talking about are not right for me.' She turned to Dave. 'Can we go, please?'

~

In the taxi, Jane snuggled in his arms.

'After all that, I'm ashamed to say I'm feeling horny,' he said, chasing the image of Gina from his mind. 'You?'

'I don't want the animal sex that Gina mentioned but I do want to make love to you.' He wondered if Jane was chastising him. 'You know, they made me feel uncomfortable too, but they never actually said the four of us should romp together. Could they have been having a genuine conversation without it being a come-on?'

'Hardly.'

Jane bolted into a sitting position. 'Do you think Sally and her boyfriend did it with them?'

'If they did, she lined us up as replacements.'

'What? No, surely not. But I obviously didn't know her that well. What about the tickets? Do we have to go and see this Clapton chap? Our seats are probably next to theirs.'

He had given the tickets to Ellen and laughingly told her why he did so. Dave turned Mart's business card over in his hand. Why had he kept it? He crushed it and threw it in the rubbish bin.

Star Quality

A production company rented a warehouse three blocks from the Coach House to make scenery and hold rehearsals for an upcoming West End play. The actors soon found the pub and made it their lunch time retreat for what they said at the outset, would be approximately six weeks.

On the day of their first appearance in the pub, the actors arrived as the lunch trade began to wane, handed Dave credit cards and asked to run individual tabs for the session. They seemed to be without time restraints and stayed at the bar from one-forty-five to around four-thirty. Once they discouraged other drinkers from remaining at the bar, they spread themselves out with their most famous member, John Cobalt at their centre. The less acclaimed actor, Michael Victor seemed happy to remain at the periphery of the group. Their conversations were interspersed with ostensibly impromptu bouts of rehearsal, during which they sometimes made sudden body movements for which other drinkers needed to beware. They were undeniably entertaining and the pub's other customers were enraptured by the presence and interplay of the celebrities

Two of the three women in the group ordered champagne by

the glass. Two men drank cocktails and another wanted only Jim Beam. When they asked to settle their tabs, they were not happy.

'I couldn't possibly have drunk this amount of alcohol!' exclaimed one inebriated actor.

'You ordered two rounds, sir,' Dave told the man. 'Plus you ordered five drinks for yourself between rounds. Here are the register slips.'

'I don't care! I want to see the licensee.'

'She isn't here at the moment. If you're unhappy with your bill, leave me a number where she can contact you. But I need you to settle the account now.'

One of the unknown actors complained, 'You're trying to take advantage of me because I'm famous.'

One woman loudly stated, 'I wouldn't have drunk so much champagne by the glass, would I? I would have ordered a bottle.'

John Cobalt looked at his bill and smiled. 'You're not the cheapest hostelry in London,' he told Dave. 'But you are clean and convenient.' He turned to the others. 'Listen chaps, this place is just what we need whilst we're rehearsing at that God-forsaken warehouse. As this is our first day, I'll pick up the tabs so there'll be no complaints.'

Some muttered 'Thank you' and a couple gushed their relief.

'May I suggest that on future occasions, we dispense with rounds? If everyone looks after him or herself, we'll all be fine. Agreed?'

'Yes.'

'Absolutely.'

'You're right.'

'Good idea.'

'That's settled then,' said the leading man as he paid the eight accounts. Dave was grateful that the unpleasant situation had ended with smiles all round and a big tip for him.

~

One or more of the actors appeared in the pub every afternoon. As word spread about the possibility of the troupe frequenting the establishment, business at the Coach House increased. Unfortunately for the customers, the well-known players did not make a second showing for over a week. When the main attraction did eventually show, it was at three o'clock and most of the fans and the curious had returned to work. It was immediately obvious that the star of *Bookworm* and *The Man from Manchester* had been imbibing elsewhere. He ogled the few women who had been able to maintain their vigil beyond the lunch hour as he strode to the bar. As Cobalt sat on a barstool in front of Ellen, a young woman arose from her seat by the window.

'Gee and tee, my good woman, if you will.'

'Ice?' Ellen asked between gritted teeth.

'Please. Plus a slice.'

The fan arrived. 'Hi, Mr Cobalt. I wondered if you'd give me your autograph.'

'That means you stopped.' The fan's face took on a blank look. 'Wondering. Did you conclude that I would?'

The look remained blank. 'I'm sorry?'

'You said you'd wondered. Therefore, you weren't still wondering when you decided to speak to me. The fact that you *did* decide to speak to me must mean that your wondering had led you to conclude that I *would* give you my autograph.'

The young woman looked questioningly at Ellen who rolled her eyeballs to the heavens.

'Well, I didn't know whether you would give me your autograph or not, Mr Cobalt. But, like my dad used to say 'if you don't ask, you don't get'.'

'True, but I understood the saying to be slightly different. My dad, as we are apparently calling our paters this day, used to say, 'Thems as don't ask, don't get, and thems as *do* ask, are too rude to get'. Have you heard that before?'

'No. Look. Are you going to give me your autograph or not?'

'Aha. We're going from obsequious to belligerent now, are we?' The fan turned and headed for the door. 'You give up too easily young lady. How about a trade?'

The young woman turned back to face the star whose brightness had dimmed. 'What kind of trade?'

'How badly do you want my autograph? Will you sleep with me to get it?'

'Never.'

'Very good. How about, let me see….mmm…how about giving me a kiss?'

'Are you serious?'

'In a way. I'm seeing what the parameters are, and then we'll start to narrow them.'

'I'd give you a kiss on your cheek.' The woman was clearly embarrassed and she shyly looked around the bar for moral support.

The big star laughed aloud. 'What are your thoughts on you and me going to the bog, where you could inspect my log?' He slapped his thigh and laughed again, 'Damn, that's good. Got to remember that one: bog and log.'

'Are you out of your mind? Your autograph was something I would have liked to have because I used to admire you. I had no idea you were such a pig of a man. You disgust me.' The woman ran out of the pub.

'Oh, how bloody dreary. It seems I've upset one of my fans.' He swivelled on the stool and faced Ellen. 'Another gee and tee, please.'

'First off, you disgust *me* too.' The blonde, frizzy-haired barmaid told the star. 'And secondly, I think you've had enough for today, sir.'

'And who are you to make such a judgement?'

'I'm the one representing my boss' interests.'

'I see…not my day for the ladies, is it? In that case I shall exit stage left, as I believe we say in the industry.'

The man still owed the price of his drink, but Ellen let him leave without further comment. She'd let everyone know what had happened (distasteful or not, it was still delicious gossip) and whoever was on duty the next time Cobalt appeared, would recoup the cost with interest.

~

Dave was working behind the bar the next time the famous actor visited the pub. The man had two 'gee and tee's and struck up a conversation with a well-dressed woman who appeared to be in her mid-thirties. The two retired to a table by the wall and, half an hour later, quietly left together.

~

Michael Victor and the rest of the cast became frequent visitors to the Coach House. They usually stayed for the entire afternoon and anyone behind the bar was always well rewarded for their work.

There had been a day when one of the troupe's unknown actors over-indulged and started to curse his mother and all others who, he claimed, were responsible for him being homosexual. His companions tried to quieten him, but eventually Dave had been compelled to ask the man to leave the pub.

~

On a Tuesday afternoon, when Dave was serving, the whole cast, the director, his assistants, script people, tradesmen and a variety of others associated with the production arrived together. The director produced his American Express card and stated that everything eaten or drunk by the group be charged to his account. 'This is our last day here,' the director shouted, 'and we aim to make it a memorable one. Next week we start dress rehearsals and two weeks after that, we open!' He screamed the word 'open' at the top of his squeaky voice and his crowd cheered with joy.

The session was hectic and as word of who was in the pub spread around the neighbourhood, the place filled. The boss called in both Jack and Ellen to help handle the rush of business. Ellen was not happy at being found at home at two in the afternoon. 'I need to get a life,' she told Dave.

Dave noticed the woman who had befriended Cobalt was present and the two again sat at a table. This time it was next to a window.

The troupe stayed well beyond their normal departure time. Regular clientele mingled with the actors and production crew. The celebrities signed autographs, told jokes and joined everyone in singing some of the popular songs from musicals in which they had acted. The more alcohol consumed; the greater the number of kisses exchanged and body parts fondled. Actors ordered drinks for customers, instructing the staff to add the cost to the director's account. When the party finally subsided, the generous director paid the thousand-pounds-plus bill without a question. He and the players then departed in limousines that had been patiently waiting in the street outside the pub. Only incidental workers remained. One of them, a carpenter, claimed to have signed five autographs. When the remaining free drinks left specifically for them dried up, they quickly left the premises. The presence of the long black automobiles outside had attracted a passing crowd and so the party atmosphere in the pub continued for quite a while after the original celebrants were long gone.

~

Dave was ten minutes early for his shift the following evening.

'Take a look at that window over there on the right wall.' Ellen told him. Dave looked across the room, but could not discern anything unusual. 'No, ya great boob. Go over there and take a look.'

Dave went to the window in question, 'Boob?'

'You know what I mean. It's a term of endearment.'

It took a couple of seconds for Dave to figure out what he was looking for. Then he saw it. Someone had etched the name John Cobalt into the glass. 'Who the hell did this?'

'Gotta assume it was the big man himself.'

'Nah. Who would do something like that? Jeez, it'd be just like kids carving their initials in a tree trunk.'

'Well, somebody clearly did it. You got any suggestions?'

'Coulda been the woman he sat with last night. It's the right table. Maybe she did it with a ring she was wearing.'

'Was she wearing a diamond ring?'

'No idea.'

'It makes no difference. The boss has been on to the Evening Standard. They're sending someone out here to take a picture of it for tomorrow's edition. She reckons we could use the publicity. Bring in more punters.'

~

People started to arrive when the doors of the pub opened at ten the next morning. The landlord had had the foresight to employ two security personnel who made sure nobody viewed the scratching without having first purchased a drink. Red velvet ropes suspended from golden poles defined the route from the end of the bar to the attraction. Punters zigzagged in line as if they were queuing for the cinema. The pub's regulars were, at first, pleased with the notoriety now associated with their local, but the enthusiasm of some of them waned when they realised their favourite room was going to be unavailable for a day or two. The weekend brought an influx of new gazers but by Sunday night the pub returned to normality.

~

On Wednesday of the following week, Dave served a woman with a half-pint of cider.

'I hear John Cobalt signed his autograph in one of your windows last week. Can I see it?'

'It's over there.' Dave pointed to the window.

The woman inspected the pane of glass and then returned to her seat. 'Do you get many celebrities in here?'

'Not really. The occasional one drops in, but I guess they're too shy of the public to visit your average pub.'

'I collect celebrity autographs.'

Dave smiled. 'So do a lot of people. We had quite a few during the period those actors were drinking here.'

'Yeah, but I'm different. I sleep with them first. I never collect an autograph of any celebrity I haven't slept with.'

'You'da had no problem with whatshisface. I understand he propositioned several young girls who asked for his moniker.'

'I wish I'd been here.'

A little later in the evening Dave served the woman with another glass of cider. 'Will you take this number and call me if anyone like that comes into this pub again?' She handed Dave a business-like card made on a personal computer. It announced the name Sharon and had coloured stars around the border.

'You mean any celebrity?'

'Yeah.'

'What about females?'

'Them too.'

'You sleep with both the males and the females?'

'Sweetheart, I'll sleep with Lassie if I have to.'

Dave threw the home-made card away. The pane of glass had been broken several weeks ago and the trickle of celebrity hounds had all but petered out.

Sunday in the Country

Jane's sister sent an invitation to a Harvest Festival at a small church in Berkshire, followed by a cocktail party to be hosted by the Pearsons. When Dave asked who the Pearsons were, Jane waived a hand in the air and said, 'Some people my family know. Apparently they're afflicted with money, not that I recall them.'

Dave drove on the outward journey because Jane knew something of the area and was therefore a better navigator on the relatively unfamiliar country roads, plus the rain might have let up by the time they returned. The arrangement suited him as it allowed him to freely imbibe at the cocktail party.

Finding the church wasn't easy. Signposts were a rare sight and they had to make several enquiries before reaching their goal.

'Do these people still worry about a German invasion?' Dave asked his girlfriend.

She laughed. 'I don't know. You'll have to ask my sister when next you see her. She won't be here this weekend, but perhaps we'll see her at Christmas.'

'Won't be there. How come the invitation?'

'It's her invitation.'

His eyebrows went up. 'We're coming down here again at

Christmas?'

Jane waffled. 'I don't know yet *what* the family's plans are this year. Would it be so bad if we were to stay with my sister and her family?'

'Is there an alternative?'

'You could stay in London.'

He was non-committal. 'So, who's the person we're seeing today?'

'Lillian Tweedie; I went to school with her. She and her children have lived down there since the divorce. It's cheaper than London and she has a charming little cottage; thatched roof, roses climbing white walls, and all that calendar picture stuff.'

'Calendar picture stuff?'

Jane punched his arm. 'You know what I mean. Those large calendars with pictures of rural England that sell well in the States and convince Americans to hop over here to see the quaint little villages that they then want to buy.'

'Buy?'

'Some do.'

'Whole villages?'

Jane laughed. 'It's true! There was some mucky-muck at work, well, our American office, who came over here and wanted to do just that. He thought that by paying enough, he could get the householders and businesses to sell their properties to him.'

'What about the church? Did the village have a church?'

'The village he eventually chose did. When somebody asked that very question, he said he'd give enough money to the Pope or the Archbishop to make them happily sell the property. He expected everyone would carry on as if nothing had changed.'

'You're having me on.'

Jane laughed again. 'I swear I'm not. The man apparently has a gazillion dollars and has traced his family roots to England. Ergo, he wants a quaint English village.'

'Did he get to buy it?'

'Nooooo, of course not.'

'Do ya think he'd be interested in a London Pub? The one where you and I met? He'd have to pay a finders' fee, of course.'

'You never know.'

~

They stopped to ask for directions to the church. 'Ah, the church at Oleowater. Go down 'ere fer a while and yer'll see a farm selling cream. Go past that fer a coupla miles and turn left. Go past 'Iggins farm and turn right. Past the Lord's place and turn left. Saint Cuthbert's be half way down the lane. You can't miss it.'

As the man used the correct name of the church, they decided he must know the best way to get there. It wasn't as if they had a visible steeple to head for. 'What did you mean by 'the Lord's place'? Jane asked him.

'Ah, that'll be Lord Forestbrown's place. Nice 'ouse. You can't miss it.'

~

The directions turned out to be remarkably clear. When they arrived, they found the church was without a spire. It did however, have a bell tower.

The rain continued. They parked as close to the church as possible, put up their umbrellas and picked their way along the uneven road, sidestepping rivulets created by dissolving droppings. There could not have been more than thirty headstones in the graveyard, most of them in a neglected state. Plastic flowers adorned one. Another had a plastic union flag somehow attached. The couple folded their umbrellas and leant them against the church wall, alongside a phalanx of others. As they entered the building, they almost collided with the sole bell-ringer; her young face screwed up in concentration as she pulled on the one bell that called local worshipers to the service. She seemed completely undeterred by the fact the place was already packed. Jane looked around for somewhere to sit and saw the only space was on the front pew. Her friend, Lillian Tweedie, sat with her children and was trying to entertain and control them. Not wanting to sit in what was obviously a reserved pew; the couple stood against the back wall.

~

The interior of the church was miniscule, probably twenty feet by eighty. The altar, sanctuary and choir stalls (which were filled with worshippers), took up approximately twenty feet of the length.

A very tall man approached Jane and Dave and suggested they might like to sit in the front pew. 'It's usually reserved for our local Lord, but I haven't seen any cars at his residence this weekend, so you might as well sit in his place'.

'Thank you,' said Dave. When seated he whispered to Jane, 'Wonder if it's the same lord referred to by the man who gave us the directions?'

'Has to be. How many lords do you think could live in a community of this size?'

Dave felt uncomfortable sitting in the conspicuous front pew, especially as Jane had asked him to wear a suit and tie for the day. The upside was that Jane was wearing an impressive outfit and some striking jewellery. Her hair shone and her understated makeup was perfect; she looked fantastic. However, he was in a church and so he fidgeted until Jane took his hand, presumably because she sensed his unease and felt clutching his mitt would prevent him from bolting.

Someone observed it had been a long time since the church had been so full.

'That's because of Pearson's cocktail party,' someone reasoned.

~

The church had no minister, priest, or vicar, so a lady who described herself as a 'lay reader' led the service. She opened with a prayer, and then a hymn. As there was no organ or any other kind of musical accompaniment, the lay reader asked a Mr. Higgins to lead the singing. He started out in a firm voice and the rest of the congregation shuffled musically along behind him. "We plough the fields and scatter the good seed on the land, and it is fed and watered by God's almighty hand."

While the congregation sang the hymn, children quietly made their way to the altar and laid baskets of fruit and vegetables at its base. One young boy took the contents from his basket and laid them loose amongst the other offerings, then returned to his seat with his empty wicker hamper. His mother blushed with embarrassment.

When the singing stopped and all children had returned to their parents, the lay reader smiled at the assembly and explained that, although fruit and vegetables were important to sustain life, water was even more essential to man, beast and plant. 'I have a small experiment I'd like to perform to give an example.' She presented three glasses containing clear liquids and asked for volunteers to taste the contents. Most adults inspected their shoes but just about every child showed admirable eagerness.

The first boy took a sip from the glass offered. 'Ugh. It tastes like salt'.

'It *is* salt!' beamed the congregation's cheerful leader.

A young girl hesitantly tasted the contents of the second glass and her hand flew immediately to her mouth and her eyes widened before her face was screwed into mask of horror. She ran to where her parents sat. 'Spit it out into your dad's handkerchief at once!' The outraged mother instructed her young daughter whilst she glared at the lay reader.

'What on earth's the matter?' the surprised lay reader said. She picked up the third glass and sniffed the contents. 'Oh dear.' She reddened. 'I am sorry, but I gave you the glass containing gin by mistake. I should have given you the pure water. Please accept my apologies.' She sent the third volunteer back to his seat.

Dave reckoned the third child would have reacted the same way, so how could the woman be surprised? 'I would've handled the gin with aplomb,' he said to Jane. 'Perhaps I should finish what's left in the glass?

'Don't even think about it,' she hissed.

'I'm afraid my experiment went a little awry,' said the reader. 'Perhaps another day? Apologies all round and especially to my young technical assistants. Let's press on and sing hymn number four-eighty-two.'

Mr. Higgins obligingly began. "All things bright and beautiful, all creatures great and small. All things wise and wonderful, the Lord God made them all."

The congregation joined in the singing. Unfortunately, Mr. Higgins had, in his enthusiasm, started the hymn in a high key. The womenfolk valiantly tried to reach the higher notes. They looked at one another, questioning whether they would be able to finish the musical glorification of their Lord. The men merely grunted the words.

One of Lillian's children, a small boy with a mass of blonde curls walked up to the lay reader singing at the top of his voice. He was too young to know the words but, as he knew the tune, he didn't allow his ignorance to hamper him. He stood next to the surprised lady, slipped his hand into hers and the two of them finished the hymn in a sort of unison. Meanwhile, mother Tweedie frantically slapped her thigh with increasing rapidity, urging her wayward child to re-join her, which he did only after the song of praise was over.

Prayers of thanksgiving followed, and then the final hymn. During the singing, two men presented collection plates at the front pews. Neither Jane nor Dave had coins. The smallest denomination in Dave's wallet was a twenty-pound note. Jane took the plate and put a ten-pound note onto the red velvet. Dave grasped the plate and picked up Jane's offering which he replaced with his larger note. Lillian Tweedie added some coins before Dave turned and passed the plate to the man in the pew behind him. The man saw the twenty-pound note, put the change he had planned to give back in his pocket and extracted his wallet. He thumbed a ten-pound note, looked again at the money already lying on the velvet, and withdrew a twenty instead. Dave suppressed a smile. Other members of the congregation on the same side of the aisle also re-thought their contribution. Wives elbowed husbands, whispered in their ears, nodded at the collection plate and urged changes of plans.

'How could you?' Jane hissed.

'What?'

'Take money from the collection plate!'

'It was only change. They did pretty well out of us. Twenty bloody quid!'

Jane pinched his thigh. 'Don't swear in church!'

'Bollocks!'

Jane lifted her hymnal to cover her laughter. Dave coughed to clear his throat and started singing the chorus of the hymn he suddenly recognised.

~

As Jane and Dave filed slowly out of the church, they overheard snippets of conversation about the two extravagant strangers in their midst. As they had sat in the front pew, they were among the last to leave the church. The unrelenting rain caused polite pandemonium at the door. People picked up uniformly black umbrellas and tried to ascertain ownership. Once reasonably confident they had the right brollies in hand, they stepped across the door-stone and into the deluge. Lillian Tweedie was already at the church gate. The Londoners had had the unwitting foresight to bring golf umbrellas that bore the logo of Jane's American employer, so they picked them up, snapped them open and followed Lillian.

~

They walked to the Pearson's house and found several mats immediately inside the front door on which everyone should wipe their feet. Many guests had brought house shoes and they stood in the rain, teetering first on one foot and then the other whilst they took off their high boots and put on their slippers, all the while holding their umbrellas aloft to keep dry. The various and often garishly coloured galoshes were left to suffer the elements, along with the umbrellas.

Their host, Mr. Pearson, turned out to be the tall man who had arranged for Dave and Jane to use the front pew at the church and he greeted them with a glass of white or rosé.

'Do you have any red?' Dave asked.

'Not this year, old chap, but the rose's quite robust, so I think it might suffice.'

'Thank you.'

'Don't mention it. Busy right now, but I'll talk to you later.'

Jane opted for the white but grimaced after she took her first sip.

Dave thought Pearson's house might be better described as a mansion. On a table in the foyer was a model of a horse made from pieces of driftwood. Impressive-looking art work covered the walls. In one room, there were pennants and other memorabilia of the Grenadier Guards. Dave found the items interesting.

'Was Mr Pearson in the guards, then?' he asked the nearest person.

'Not mister, old boy. No titles or Christian names for the men here. No need for 'em, what'.

'I suppose not. Wilson.' Dave offered his hand to the man.

'Parker.' He took Dave's hand. 'Delighted. Yes, Pearson was in the Grenadiers. Got his majority but had to pack it in. Family and business, ya know. Had to take up the family reins after his father died. Estates and all that gubbings. Last thing he did was to be 'senior officer of horse' at the Trooping of the Colour. Splendid chap. Trouble was, his height made his poor horse look so bloody small, called it his donkey.'

~

Lillian joined them. 'You caused quite a stir in church.' She grinned. 'This lot,' she tipped her head backwards to indicate she included everyone at the party, 'never like to be outdone by strangers. Well done! The church needs you to attend more often.'

'The church won't be as lucky next time, believe me,' Dave said with a laugh.

~

The pair continued to circulate until a short, stocky man stopped them. He had the ruddy complexion of a farmer and the veined nose of a drinker. 'Day to you.' He offered his hand. 'You be that accountant chappie I'm s'posed to meet? Going to tell me what to do with me blasted money?'

'Er, no,' said Dave as he shook the man's hand.

'Damn. Royal pain. Have to get rid of eight million by October or the bloody government'll become me partner. 'S'too much. Blasted Europeans.' Jane stood out of the man's eye line and looked aghast at Dave. He ignored her attempt to make him smile and politely sympathised with the man who, thankfully, didn't notice her antics. 'Here, take me card. Call me to make a new appointment, there's a good chap.'

~

Jane had disappeared in search of something better to drink when Dave bumped into Pearson 'Everything okay?' the man asked

'Fine,' Dave replied. 'I understand that you were in the guards. See any action?'

'Yes, actually, the Gulf War.'

'Really. I always wondered why the Allies didn't go on and take

Baghdad.'

'Didn't want to run the place for the next ten years. No fun in occupying an Arab city…or any foreign city, come to that. Lack of a social life you know.' He smiled. 'What do you think of the wine?'

'Not bad. You were right about the rose; it is more like a blush. How come no red?'

'Good question! My cousin makes the stuff. Has a chateau in the Dordogne and suffered a disaster with the red a few years ago. Grapes were harvested last year, but the wine's not up to snuff yet. Some bug or other. There was another reason but I'm damned if I can remember what it was. Left the others pretty much intact, strangely. We're the sole UK distributor, so look for the stuff in your local wine shop and buy some.'

'Will do,' Dave lied.

'Here's me card, or at least me vintner's card. Wear too many hats these days. Life was much more organised in the service.' His face brightened. 'What did you think of our church?' He didn't wait for an answer. 'S'our pride and joy. Of course, being without a minister's a bit inconvenient. We have to apply to the local bishop whenever we want a service. He invariably sends someone along, but it's always on his terms. Slightly like the American circuit court really. We have no gas or electricity, which can be rather amusing at Christmas. We put candles on the tree and light them for the service. Always take a fire extinguisher.' Dave hoped his smile was appropriate. 'Our lay reader today had to leave in a hurry as she had another gig. Interesting gel. She and her husband used to be missionaries in India. Now they go round doing these gigs. Often have one or the other of them, even though we only have about six services a year. By the way, magnificent gesture for the collection. Made a few of us recalculate our offerings!'

Dave wondered how many people had seen him take the ten-pound note. 'What's the story with the front pew?' he enquired.

'Ah, Lord Forestbrown. Local celeb. Ex government minister farmed out with a title. Useful man to have around.'

Mrs. Pearson continuously made the rounds with a bottle in each hand, filling up empty and partially empty glasses.

Dave talked to an old lady who wanted him to know that India was the only place left on earth where an Englishwoman of fixed income could live reasonably well.

When Pearson's young daughter, the campanologist, meandered amongst the guests with a tray of cocktail sausages, Dave took just one, feeling it would be selfish to take more in the presence of the lady with the fixed income.

Mrs. Pearson came by again. 'Do you have any idea how hard it is to find a decent riding instructor for my children?' she wanted Dave to know as she filled his glass. 'Nobody knows a good horse when they see one these days.' His sympathetic smile encouraged the woman. 'And don't even start me on domestics! Our two volunteered their time to do whatever volunteers do at the harvest festival. I understand they're distributing produce and whathaveyou to the hospitals et al. That's why I'm doubling as the wine waiter and Alexandra is carrying the sausages around. I wouldn't mind but it's my time they're volunteering. Do you have the same problems in London?'

Dave shook his head. 'No, I've not been subjected to that kind of thoughtlessness.'

~

When sausages were no longer offered, everyone realised it was time to leave. So much for being able to imbibe with reckless abandon, Dave thought. And still it rained. At the door there was modest mayhem over umbrellas. Some upended their Wellington boots to pour rain water out. He and Jane retrieved their bumbershoots, gave an all-encompassing farewell and left. Twenty minutes later, they found a pub with decent wine and good food in substantial proportions. Dave risked Jane's anger by commenting on the people they'd met.

She laughed. 'This is Berkshire Dave and they're the country set. They think they set the social rules for around here. For what it's worth, I agree with you but we all have to get on with each other don't we.'

Dave flipped the multimillionaire's card toward the rubbish bin but missed. Given that he and Jane were committed to each other, he might possibly meet him again. However, as he was not about to buy the man's wine, he saw no reason to keep his business card.

'Tis the Season

Dave unfolded a rectangle of pale-yellow paper that had on it a number he couldn't place. The thin sheet could only have come from a Christmas cracker. He turned it over and looked at the number scribbled in pencil on the back. He had no idea who the number belonged to but he surmised he must have acquired it at a Christmas function so it had to be at least a year old. The pub's spacious 'back room' hosted a large number of private company parties every year, whilst other group celebrations arrived in the main bar on an impromptu basis.

At the onset of every holiday season, both the brewery and the landlord of the Coach House sent memos to all members of permanent and temporary staff, telling them that a 'hands off the customers' policy was mandatory. Despite the threats contained in the memo, there were still 'incidents' every year. Dave believed he would have definitely recalled any woman's number that he had received just a few days earlier, so the number he held had to be at least a year old. But if that were the case, why hadn't he either recorded the number or thrown it away last year? What had been so special about this telephone number? The area code indicated the owner was from out of town but that didn't serve to jog his memory.

If some gorgeous female had given it to him, he would surely remember her. He ordered a pint from Jack and tried to recall what had happened at last year's parties.

~

A company of insurance brokers had been shocked when their well-oiled senior accountant gave every employee a list of how much money each department head had to distribute as bonuses amongst his underlings. Those from the Marine department, each of whom had been awarded two weeks pay, were further upset when the accountant told them their boss had assigned himself the amount needed for a down payment on his new home somewhere in Surrey. The department head's wife was at the bar telling a friend about the new house she and her husband had closed on that day. She became upset when one of her husband's aggrieved underlings asked her what it was like to be married to a pimp.

'Who do you think you're talking to,' the woman squeaked in a haughty manner.

'You! Every time you put your key in the front door of your new home, I want you to think of how your husband screwed the people that work with him so he could scrape together the down payment for it.'

The woman rose and called for her husband, who was deep in conversation with his boss. 'Geoffrey! Do something about this man. He's being extremely rude to me.'

The man wasn't deterred at the sight of Dave shaking his head. 'Shall we have a race?' the disgruntled employee asked her. 'See if you or dear Geoffrey can get to the MD before me. D'ya think Geoffrey is worth more than the whole department?'

'Enough,' Dave told him. 'You've made your point. How about I pour you another drink?'

The head of the three-person industrial property department received one-and-a-half million pounds. He waved the notice in the air. 'One-and-a-half-million, chaps!' He turned around, making sure everyone in the room was aware of his success. 'To my terrific Girl Friday, Wendy, I give half-a-million!' The thirty-something year old woman broke down in tears. 'To my assistant, John, I give half-a-million.' The man turned ashen and made for the bathroom to presumably regurgitate his turkey and trimmings. The 'Girl-Friday' had given Dave her number earlier in the evening, but after she learned of her new economic status, she wound up going home arm in arm with her nouveau riche co-worker. She had quietly asked Dave not to call her and he had obligingly thrown her number away.

When the party broke up at eleven, Dave learned the MD had fired the accountant, Geoffrey and the disgruntled employee from the Marine department. It was then he had realised the pair and their wives had been absent for a while.

At another party, a young secretary had found that removing her tights and panties improved her chances of winning the limbo competition. Jack had taken a photograph of the woman as she slid under the bar when it was at its lowest level. The managing director of the company had paid him twenty-five pounds for the film. The race to get the young woman's telephone number had been so great that Dave had decided not to compete. The photograph had appeared on the Internet two or three days later.

~

The owner of a local bookstore suddenly realised, after four glasses of Tio Pepe, that Dave's smile was the reason she had left Leicester more than a decade ago. Once the food and speeches had been digested, the lady perched on a barstool and watched her minions play their games. Dave smiled for her so much that his cheeks had begun to ache. She made it up to him later, but he remembered her as 'one night stand' material only. He was reasonably sure it wasn't her number on the piece of paper, but he did ask Jack to pass him the telephone directory so he could check if the area code was for Leicester. He considered checking the area codes for the whole country but when he saw how many there were, he decided a forgotten face was not worth the trouble involved.

Dave was pleased to remember Sergei had attended a recent bash hosted by the Silver Fox. The inventor was accompanied by a woman Dave knew by sight and the two had often been seen together in the Coach House since.

A woman who owned a small trucking company had hosted a large celebration in the back room. Her offices were in the eastern suburbs of Greater London but her employees had persuaded her to 'go up west' for their annual party. The drivers found the Coach House by folding a map of London in half and picking a pub that mirrored their office location. A representative group of truckers had apparently spent a night pub-crawling the area and had reported to their boss that the Coach House was the kind of place where they would like to start the evening. They had not foreseen that their employer would hire a room and were not ecstatic at her decision to do so.

'Can't we move the bleedin' parhy tuh da bar?' one of them had asked.

'After we've eaten and I've handed out the bonuses you can do whatever you like. That will be the end of my participation in the party.'

The man had grinned suggestively. 'You're gonna to miss all the fun.'

'Yes, I'm sure. Strippers, fights and great quantities of alcohol. Am I right?'

The grin turned into a guffaw. 'You're not far off!'

'Thanks, but no thanks.'

The drivers had drunk so many pints of beer that Dave, who with a waitress, was working the party alone, had a hard time pulling them fast enough. Their boss ordered a bottle of wine which she drank sparingly.

Once the turkey and trimmings had been devoured, the owner of the company stood and called out names of men who stepped up to receive their envelope of Christmas cheer. As far as Dave could see, some men received cash, others cheques and a few received some kind of financial statement. Each one seemed to get an explanation of what was in the envelope. Some men grinned or pumped the air with a fist after inspecting their envelopes' contents. Three of them could not contain themselves and let out a 'Fuckin' Ay!' Others appeared disappointed or unhappy.

When the last man had opened his envelope, the party began to break up. Some men left their coats and jackets in the room whilst they went to the public bar for a few more pints before leaving for the 'West End'.

'Too bleedin' early yet. Might as well 'ave a few more free ones 'ere.'

Others had thought the time was perfect to phone for taxis to take them to 'Raymond's Revue Bar'.

The owner had taken her bottle of wine to the bar and lifted herself wearily onto one of the barstools. 'Keeping this lot happy is a full time job. Are they okay drinking in the public bar?'

'Sure, as long as they know that they'll have to pay for their drinks. Your tab is still in effect in here, but it can't be transferred.'

'Don't worry about it. Whatever money I put behind this bar that isn't used, is for you and the waitress. You both did a good job. You must be exhausted.'

'Thanks. I was half expecting some trouble when you were handing out the bonuses. Some guys were happy with the contents of their envelopes, but some of the others were downright miserable.'

'It's all up to them. I don't really give them a bonus. With three pence in the pound profit, I'm lucky to keep my head above water. All employees, including drivers, have the option of saving a percentage of their pay in a money market account. Some put a tidy sum away and they like getting a cheque or a statement of account every year. Some spend the year withdrawing the money so they can piss it up against a wall. Others take the money out to pay for a vacation or whatever other foolishness they can think of; a better car, a bigger television, whatever. So, there are those that are sad and those that are glad.'

'Sounds like a tough job, running your business.'

'You have no idea. Every one of them thinks he's the world's greatest gift to women. Why do you think none of the girls from the office is here? I have to take them out for a night on the town without the drivers. There are days when I half wish I was older and uglier. Thankfully, most everybody worked for my late father, God rest his soul, and some of the respect they had for him has rubbed off on me. Then there are the drinkers. I have to make as sure as I can that they're fit to drive when they turn up in the morning. The union won't allow me to breathalyse them, so I have to use my judgement. If I consider a driver unfit to work, he loses a day's pay. That can get ugly.' The woman indicated that she needed another drink. 'I've had enough wine. Do you have some cognac in here?'

'I will have. Can you hang on while I get a bottle from the main bar?' He returned in less than a minute. He found a snifter not used for quite some time and washed it before pouring a generous measure of the liquid.

'How much is that?'

'Nothing. I think you've got the bottle covered.'

'Thanks. The stress of the job gets to me. When four o'clock comes round…well, there are mornings I feel like turning over and going back to sleep. I get the shakes when I turn my car into the yard and it takes a couple of strong coffees to settle myself. Imagine taking coffee to settle the shakes.' The woman laughed once down her nose. 'I should take the stuff intravenously. Thank God I don't have to work again until the second of Jan. I've got some time to recharge my batteries and get my act together again.'

'Are you going away?'

'No. There's plenty to do at home and I've got a whole lot of bookkeeping to catch up on. I just need to get a lot of sleep, some good food and some good sex… and to wear a dress every day.' She looked up at Dave. 'Wearing long pants when you have legs as good as mine is a sin.' She looked at her snifter and twirled it. She raised her head to look Dave in the eye and brought the glass to her lips. 'How are you fixed for the sex part?' The words sounded strange, echoing round the voluminous snifter. 'Wanna give it a whirl? See if we fit?'

Dave had dated the woman a few times before she returned to work. Moira, her name suddenly entered his head. Moira had ended their relationship. She had told him that she had, out of necessity, to re-erect her high and hard emotional barriers. He had been about to finish their affair himself, as he hadn't noticed the barriers had been lowered. He didn't have her number recorded anywhere, but he knew the number on the slip of paper didn't belong to her.

~

There was a party where someone decided to play a game with the coat-disks. The cloakroom system consisted of two like-numbered disks for each coat hanger. The owner of the garment kept one disk while the second one remained on the hanger. The party had been a large one; one hundred and eight people. The kitchen had complained bitterly that the booking was too large to allow them to adequately prepare food for the party, as well as an unknown number of the pub's other customers. Ellen had worked with Dave behind the bar and they had experienced considerable difficulty in serving everybody in a timely manner. Thankfully, the brokerage firm's employees had endured the wait for their drinks with grace. Company personnel from a number of offices in different towns and cities across the country were present. People arrived and left at different times, but Dave had been too busy to notice the comings and goings.

The company had opted for Thai food, rather than the traditional Christmas fare. Between the main course and dessert, company hierarchy made their obligatory self-congratulatory speeches. At around nine o'clock, a couple from Scotland felt they had put in a long enough appearance and, after making the politically correct good-byes and good wishes, went to the cloakroom to retrieve their coats.

'This is not my coat,' a strident Scots female voice insisted.

'Calm down, my dear. Neither is this mackintosh mine. Just relax and let me sort it out.'

The man had made his way to the bar and asked to speak to whoever was in charge.

'That'll be me,' Dave told the man.

'The numbers we were given for our coats are wrong. Is there someone who can help us sort it out?'

'I'm afraid not, sir. Your company chose not to hire a cloakroom attendant. You took care of the matter yourselves.'

The company representative in charge of the party strode to the bar.

'What's up, Angus?'

'Our cloakroom disks dinna match the disks on the coat hangers. We've got someone else's coats.'

'I see. Leave it to me. We'll have this sorted immediately.'

The man went to the top table and announced the cloakroom disks had somehow got mixed up and the only way to sort it out was to have everyone check their garments as he called out their disk numbers. 'Will those people with disks numbered one to twenty please check their respective coat hangers now.'

A dozen people made their way to the cloakroom.

'I'm waiting. Numbers one to twenty, if you would be so kind.'

The face of a woman who had been talking turned red as she got to her feet and apologised before making her way to the cloakroom.

'Some people have already left,' someone called out. 'How will we know what their disk numbers were?'

'If they said nothing, we'll assume they had the correct disks,' the man replied with a hopeful tone of voice.

Five people returned to the room with coat hangers containing garments unknown to them. The rightful owners took charge of the coats and draped over the backs of their chairs. Three people re-entered the room with their own coats luckily espied on other hangers. The remaining five were still searching in the dimly lit closet.

Forty-five minutes later, all but three of the people present had reclaimed their own clothing. A search in the pockets of the unclaimed coats failed to reveal the identity of the owners. Seventeen people had already departed before the cloakroom catastrophe was discovered. Some of the partygoers began a game in which they tried to guess which of their seventeen co-workers already departed were wearing the wrong coats.

A redheaded man loudly complained, 'My mac was brand new and all of these are fairly worn. Whoever has my coat, has to know it, unless he was so sozzled he couldn't see straight.'

A woman who had had the foresight not to leave her silver fox coat in the cloakroom settled onto a bar stool and quietly identified the leading characters to Dave and Ellen as she provided a running commentary of the farce. 'People entrust us with untold millions to invest on their behalf. I wonder how many would pull their portfolios, if they were to witness this little cock-up?'

The party atmosphere soon evaporated and the employers and employees clutched their coats and headed out the door toward some waiting taxis or the tube station. Caroline of the silver fox fur coat had agreed to wait for Dave to finish cleaning the glasses, clearing the tables and sweeping the floor. The morning cleaners would take care of details. He dated her three times before her obsession with her fur coat and a large pear-shaped diamond ring had driven him off.

He knew the number he held in his hand was not hers.

There had been plenty of other parties, but he knew he was never going to work out who had given him the number. Was the person mad at him for not calling her? Had he called her and forgotten all about it? Could the number belong to a regular, who had perhaps returned home for Christmas and invited him to visit? He fervently hoped not! Should he throw it away or would he one day have instant recall when one of the most beautiful women he had ever seen walked in the bar? Even if she did, what could he say to her? 'Hey. You probably don't remember me but….'

And, in any case, there was Jane. He screwed the paper and dropped it in the bin.

Original Art

Dave wasn't keen to attend the Fitness Professionals' annual dinner-dance but he tried to adopt an enthusiastic attitude. He thankfully didn't have to wear a monkey suit, but Jane insisted he be the designated driver so she could let her hair down.

Bill, her assistant at the corporate gymnasium, and his balding wife, Connie, met them in the foyer. They sipped glasses of insipid sherry, and the two women tried to outdo each other with the latest snippets of celebrity gossip. Bill and Dave stood dutifully silent and nodded at people who looked at them.

Another couple joined them and Dave tried to discuss Manchester City's chances of winning the title, but everyone became churlish and he concluded they were United fans.

Jane rubbed a trace of Connie's lipstick from his cheek. 'Enough with the football talk, darling. Pick a subject everybody knows something about.'

'Weapons of mass destruction?' He raised his eyebrows questioningly.

'What do you think?'

'Religion?'

'You're a professed atheist.'

'Who better to pull apart the world's religions?'

'Come on, darling. Let's make it a subject everyone can contribute to.'

'We're down to the tele and movies then, are we?'

'They'll do for now.'

Bill wore a grin that worried Connie. 'Don't you give him any encouragement!' she hissed.

~

Once the mass-produced beef and chicken dinners were eaten, fit women in skimpy, tight-fitting dresses moved from table to table selling raffle tickets. Non-designated drivers attempted to anaesthetise themselves against the torture of the pending speeches while half-a-dozen couples moved gracefully around the shiny dance floor.

The band stopped playing and the president of Southern Fitness Professionals rose unsteadily from his chair.

'We've enjoyed a wonderful year,' he slurred. 'Let me give you the headlines and then I'll fill in the details. Thirty-six new paid-up members have joined our ranks and the golf outing was a great success, especially the nineteenth hole.' He guffawed and looked up from his notes. 'Last year's Christmas dance actually made money and the trip to The Isle of Wight was enjoyed by seventeen members who, I think,' he surveyed the room, 'are all in attendance tonight. We donated three-hundred-and-fifty pounds to the *Free Hostel for Stranded Australian Back-packers*, and...' Dave tuned out for the rest of their achievements.

~

Applause brought him back. 'Right,' he thought. 'Now the raffle and we're gonzo.' He was wrong. A personal trainer from Manchester told the Fitness Professionals how wonderful they were. Then a representative of the Action Committee told of the good works she and her fellow members had performed. Someone who looked too young to drink put his glass of beer on the table and walked to the podium to report on the successes of various teams and individuals in amateur sports.

The chair then loomed again like a bear rising on its back legs. 'Not too many of you asleep, I see. I must be getting better at this.'

There was polite laughter and a smatter of applause. 'Thank you, thank you. Let me now hand the microphone to Tommy, who, after you've had the opportunity to stretch your legs on the dance floor, will organise the drawing of the raffle.' Polite applause grew to a crescendo of relief.

~

Jane asked Dave to dance. He shuffled his feet to the slow numbers and managed to avoid her toes. When the tempo increased, he started to gyrate to the beat.

'Not bad, considering you're sober,' she remarked. 'Just keep it at this level. I don't want you going ape on me when they play some rock.'

Back at their table, Dave separated raffle tickets from their restraining staples and spread them on the white tablecloth. Lines of blue, pink, purple and yellow slips of numbered paper, sorted in descending numerical order, lay before him.

'What are the prizes?' Bill asked.

As if on cue, Tommy spoke. 'Thank you ladies and gentlemen. The members have generously donated these wonderful items for tonight's raffle. We have a wicker-work picnic basket packed with a tablecloth, matching napkins, cutlery and unbreakable stemware.' A round of applause caused him to pause. He lowered the microphone and smiled to all corners of the room. When the clapping abated, he continued. 'Another prize is this beautiful work of art, painted and donated by Eve Butterworth. It would add brightness to any room,' he said without exaggeration. The unframed oil was of pink carnations in a yellow vase on a blue table next to a green wall. The applause lacked enthusiasm. 'The last prize is a bottle of fine, single-malt, twenty-year-old scotch.'

Dave looked at Jane, mouthed 'mine' and tapped his chest. She smiled indulgently.

The picnic basket went to a brown, wrinkled woman. When she returned to her table, the applause waned and Tommy moved on.

'The winning ticket for the second prize is purple eighty-seven. Eight seven.'

And there it was, right at the head of Dave's purple line. He grinned at Jane. 'I think I'll take the scotch.'

'Don't you dare,' she whispered menacingly. 'Eve Butterworth was one of my partners in the gym we owned. She'll be mortified if you don't take it. You'll accept it with a show of gratitude.'

'You must be joking. The thing's hideous. Look at the lovely amber colour of the scotch.'

'The painting.'

'The scotch.'

'If you want *any* sex for the next month,' Jane delivered her coup-de-grace, 'you'll accept the painting.'

Diners at the table looked at Dave with sympathy.

~

When friends of the couple came to dinner two weeks later, Dave showed them the painting. 'Umm,' said Humphrey Simms, 'Working at the gallery allows me to assess all kinds of paintings but this one's a challenge.

'It's hideous,' said Jane. 'We can't wait to give it to someone next Christmas.'

'And yet we took it when we could have accepted a twenty-year-old single-malt Scotch,' Dave said sarcastically. Jane gave him an insincere smile.

Humphrey placed the still unframed oil on the table in front of him. 'It's a very amateurish effort.' He inspected the side of the canvas. 'Hang on. I think there's another painting beneath.' He fished in a pocket and extracted a penknife to scrape away some paint. 'Look. There's definitely something under these carnations. Oh, this is very exciting! Can I take it with me and do some tests? You need to be sure,' Humphrey advised Jane. 'Once we lift the carnations, we won't be able to put them back.'

~

Later, in bed, Jane snuggled up to Dave and playfully tugged his chest hair. 'Do you think Humphrey will discover an old and priceless masterpiece under those carnations?' she asked.

He smiled wistfully in the dark. 'It'd be nice, wouldn't it? We could move to Monaco, which, I believe, is a very nice haven for tax exiles.'

Jane's hand started to inch its way south. 'Aren't you glad you didn't take that bottle of scotch now?'

~

A few weeks later, Humphrey returned for dinner and brought the wrapped canvas with him. Once armed with a glass of wine, he told them, 'Bad luck, I'm afraid. It seems the same artist painted the picture beneath the pink carnations. It's of a house and garden and is worse than the flowers. The artist obviously didn't want to spring for a new canvas and painted over the original work. I know some say any art is still art, but this artist certainly had considerable front, donating the carnations as a prize.'

'No worse than me submitting my short stories to every Tom, Dick and Harry,' Dave said.

'Nothing under the house, I suppose?' Jane asked hopefully.

'No, just the canvas. We did lift the complete carnation thing so you now have a new painting to hang.'

'Oh well, it was enjoyable to fantasise about what we would have done with all that money.' Jane looked at Dave and smiled, then turned to the art curator. 'Thanks for taking the trouble, Humphrey. Do we owe you anything?'

'No. We don't get too many opportunities to lift a painting. Sorry if I got your hopes up.'

'We knew it was unlikely,' said Dave. 'Another glass of wine, Humph?'

~

Once they were in bed, Dave had an idea. 'You should tell the organisers of the Fitness Professionals dance we wish to donate another of Eve Butterworth's paintings to be raffled. You can add that this particular painting was in an art gallery for a while. That should get everyone's attention, even elevate it to first prize.'

Jane giggled. 'I can't. Can you imagine how she'd feel?'

Dave grinned evilly in the safety of darkness. 'Oh yes!'

Jane hadn't allowed him to offer the painting to the physical jerks club and so they gave it to Humphrey once more so he could lift the second work and gain a blank canvas. Humphry later told him, in September, that Eve had paid a gallery to exhibit several of her paintings and an inebriated art critic had savaged her work. People reacted strongly to the cruel assessment by buying the oils and now

'Our Eve's Art', as a local rock star had tagged the works, was in demand. They weren't worth a great deal of money and Dave hoped their appeal would fade, not wanting to one day realise he had destroyed a valuable Eve Butterworth original. He decided to keep Humphrey's business card as, provided Eve's paintings didn't start selling for tens of thousands of pounds, it would be a pleasant memory to enjoy when he one day found the card amongst his 'keepables'.

The Spirit of Christmas

Jane and Dave returned for Christmas to the Berkshire village where, in autumn, they had attended the Harvest Festival. It was again raining as they left London and splashed down the motorway towards Oleowater. The carol service at Saint Cuthbert's church was to begin at three on Christmas Eve and so the pair arrived at Jane's sister's house at two. The rain was still descending in a torrent when Dave parked in front of the house, stepped out of the car and pulled on the bell-rod.

Not wishing to get her feet wet from the splashing drops, Jane's sister, Ann stood as far back from the doorstep as she could and bade the couple welcome. 'Bring in your bags,' she invited. 'Malcolm's still at work so we'll have to go to church without him.'

Dave opened the boot of Jane's car and realised he needed to provide a cover for the supermarket-sized carton of presents, or the wrappings would get soaked. It had taken the two of them hours to surround the odd shaped gifts in bright paper, ribbons and bows, plus the attachments of little plastic penguins, miniature furry teddy bears and name tags. He unzipped his overnight bag while the rain pelted his back, soaking him through to his skin. The first available item to adequately do the job was a shirt. Two down, two to go. He slammed the boot lid shut with his elbow and dashed into the house. Guy and Annabel, Ann and Malcolm's children, were waiting in the hall.

'Ooh, you're so wet,' observed five year old Guy as he touched Dave's back.

'What's in the box?' three year old Annabel wanted to know.

'Yes, I am a bit wet.' Dave agreed with the mop-haired boy. 'None of your business,' he grinned at the impish girl.

'I bet it's Christmas presents.'

~

Dave carried the box and his bag up the stairs to the bedroom assigned to him and Jane. His girlfriend took the two wet shirts and put them on hangers to dry, hopefully without too many creases. Dave towelled and combed his hair, put on a clean dry shirt and the rain jacket he had washed the day before.

'Remind me to pack this in a more accessible place, next time.'

~

The five got into Ann's people carrier as quickly as possible, but securing young children safely in their seats is not a procedure accomplished with haste. All three adults had their lower backs exposed as they strapped the youngsters into their harnesses. Ann drove as near to Lord Forestbrown's house as she could and parked the car. Dave and Jane's backs were again exposed as they unstrapped Guy and Annabel and lifted them out of the car while Ann gathered the accessories that always accompanied the children Dave reflected ruefully on how cold the rain was.

The five walked to the church along a road awash with rainwater and country debris.

Annabel was not happy. 'Lift me up,' she screamed, her arms raised in the air. Dave picked her up and tried to hold her in a way that would keep her already dirty shoes away from his red rain-jacket. Guy looked at the road's surface with distaste but, as there were other boys of his age in the vicinity, he held his peace.

Ann grimaced. 'The joys of a rural retreat.'

As they entered the church, Dave felt Annabel stiffen in his arms. 'Mummy. Mummy. I want my mummy.'

Dave handed her over to Ann. The child no longer in his arms, he noticed the brown stains at his right hip. 'At least her shoes are clean now,' he told Ann.

Ann noticed the discolouration of his jacket. 'I'm sorry.'

'Think nothing of it. I'll just put it through the wash again.'

~

The church was aglow with red and white candles, their yellow flames flickering in a multitude of draughts. A Christmas tree festooned with live candles stood by the pulpit. The place was full and it was obvious they would not be able to sit together. Ann spied space for two at mid-point in the nave. She led Guy to the pew and sat next to him with Annabel on her lap.

The girl was still unhappy. 'I want to go home,' she mournfully repeated.

Her mother tried to placate her. 'Look at the tree. Isn't it pretty?'

Mr. Sargant strode into the church with the air of a man ready to take charge. Under his right arm, he carried a fire extinguisher. Some folks the Sargants knew slid along their pew like a folding concertina to made room for the man's wife and daughter. He took up his station by the tree and placed his extinguisher on the floor, between his feet. Mr. Higgins, also with a fire extinguisher, took up position in the centre of the building.

The local bishop had dispatched a temporary vicar to manage the Christmas service. The man must have been waiting for the arrival of the fire brigade as a signal to start, and he now made his way to the altar. Jane and Dave stood at the back wall of the building, alongside three other congregationalists.

'I thought you said the house was going to be a mess,' Dave whispered to Jane. 'The place is bloody immaculate.'

'I know. Ann had some people in to clean the place for Christmas. The poor kids are living under the threat of death if they so much as leave an empty cup anywhere until after Santa has been.'

The service opened with the hymn, *Once in Royal David's City* and Annabel perked up immediately. A boy dressed in his Sunday clothes read a passage from the bible and then the congregation sang, *While Shepherds Watched Their Flocks by Night.* A young man provided the musical accompaniment on his flute. Dave droned out the words until they reached the line *The Heavenly Babe You There*

Shall Find, to Human View Displayed. His mental image of Pamela Andersen standing naked at the altar improved his pitch considerably.

Sargant's daughter read another passage from the bible and then the vicar asked the children to go to the altar to sing, Away in a Manger.

Annabel was scooting down the aisle before the vicar finished the invitation. As she got half way, she suddenly realised she was alone and turned to look for her brother. 'Come on Guy,' she pleaded, her arm stretched out, fingers curling and uncurling with impatience. Several people laughed, making her aware of her situation. She turned and ran back to her mother, almost jumping into Ann's lap. Her big brother then took her hand and the two of them walked to the altar in the company of the other children. Lillian Tweedie's young son, resplendent in a charcoal grey suit, dark blue shirt and red bow-tie, marched up to the vicar and grasped his left hand, leaving only the right with which the man could direct the seating of the children.

Three pimply boys who considered themselves too old to join the children at the altar, but who were also nervous that some adults might not agree, slowly sank to the flag-stones and made themselves as inconspicuous as possible. After the completion of the carol, when the children were wending their way back to their parents, the three lads sheepishly stood up. Emboldened by their success, they started to blow gently at some of the candles to test the flames. As the whole assembly sang the next carol, O Little Town of Bethlehem, the boys' confidences grew and they blew a little harder, successfully extinguishing a couple of flames and then nervously looked around to see if anyone had noticed the reduced lighting. One boy made eye contact with Dave and immediately chose to inspect the ancient floor. Two men strode up to the boys, grasped an earlobe each and frog-marched the pair out of the church. People nodded their approval.

When the congregation sang, *How Silently, How Silently; The Wondrous Gift is Given*, Mr. Higgins fumbled his fire extinguisher. The red canister made a loud metallic thunk as it hit the stone floor. Most singers stuttered but then picked up the next syllable without difficulty. Higgins looked about like a nervous boy before he stooped to pick up his charge.

Unlike his previous visit, Dave was ready for the collection plate with four one-pound coins in his pocket. As the assembly sang Hark. The Herald-Angels Sing he watched a young girl, whose job it was to collect the offerings, stand at the end of each pew and wait for the silver salver to pass along the row of worshippers.

Jane suddenly became aware of her sister making small but urgent motions to attract her attention. She went up the aisle to her sister's side.

'I don't have any money for collection,' Jane said frantically. 'Malcolm usually takes care of these things, but I forgot he wasn't here yet. Do you have three pounds?'

Jane returned to Dave. 'How much money do you have on you?' she demanded. 'Don't look at me like that. I didn't bring my handbag with me as I didn't think I'd need it.' Dave reached in his pocket, then held his four one-pound coins in the palm of his open hand. Jane took three and delivered them to her sister a half-second before the collection plate reached her.

The man next to Dave had seen the exchange. 'Do you have any more change?' he asked. 'I don't have a penny on me.'

Dave gave him his last coin. His wallet revealed the lowest denomination of currency to be a ten-pound note. He felt annoyed, trapped and embarrassed at once more being caught in the same situation in front of the same group of strangers. He gave Jane his sole ten-pound note and, after again depositing a twenty in the salver, considered taking some change. He resisted the temptation but thought about how his first visit to the church had cost him twenty pounds and the current visit had thus far cost him thirty-four pounds. It was a lot of money. He faithfully promised his wallet he would never bring it into the cold stone building again.

~

After the service was over, the congregation filed out of the church and into the rain. There was a logjam at the door as people tried to find their umbrellas, but Dave, Jane and the Bellamys were unaffected, having brought no such protection with them. Dave again carried Annabel as they forced their way up the slight incline and against the tide of brown water that cascaded down the cobbled road towards them. By the time they reached Lord Forestbrown's house, they were soaked anew. As everyone shed their outer clothing, Dave noticed the rain had soaked through the material of his waterproof jacket. He twisted his arm around his cold back and discovered his shirt was wet. Ann set the children loose with some of their friends and the adults joined the wine line.

~

Lady Forestbrown, their host's mother, stood by a table covered with glasses containing white or rose wine. Dave wondered about the lack of red wine and concluded Sargent's products were again on offer.

Mr. Higgins joined them, wearing a dirty shirt with a frayed collar beneath an unwashed sweater, the fire extinguisher still under his arm. He was having a difficult time keeping control of the appliance, holding his glass of wine and shaking hands. When he saw the food at another table, he hastily deposited the red canister in the corner of the room and armed himself with a sausage roll.

'He's unbelievable,' said Ann as she almost imperceptibly shook her head from side to side. 'I heard he takes the shirt and sweater off as one garment. He lives with his mother in the large farmhouse you might have seen just before you turned right onto the road where we live. The untidy lady at the church with four children is his common-law wife. Apparently, mother Higgins doesn't think the woman is good enough for her son, so she stays in a minute cottage that stands back from the main house. It was originally meant to house a farm worker, not a woman with four children! And she's pregnant with their fifth child, poor woman. You couldn't blame her if she prayed every night for the matriarch's demise. The old battle-axe must be well into her eighties.'

~

Mr. Bagalot (Bah-gay-low) found Dave. 'I say, aren't you that accountant chappie that helped me invest me money?'

Dave shook his head. 'No.'

'Really? Just recommended you to Jones. You sure?'

'That I'm not an accountant?'

'Suppose you'd know. Dashed inconvenient. Got to tell Jones I was wrong now.' He turned his head as if surveying the room in search of Jones. His hunt must have been in vain because he turned his attention back to Dave. 'Got me a herd of stud bulls scattered from Lands End to John 'O Groats. Damn fine investment. Saved me all kinds of money. Damn fine job. First time I ever made money out of sex. Usually costs me, what.' He made a suggestive guffaw for the whole room to hear. 'Someone suggested I might like to invest me money in oil, but I can't stand the filthy stuff. Leave it to the Arabs, I say. 'Course the bloody Europeans'll probably find a law against the cattle deal sooner or later. Move on to something else then, what.'

~

The lady with the fixed income hadn't yet been forced to take up residence in India. 'How are you, Mister Wilson?' she inquired.

Dave was amazed that she knew his name, let alone remembered it. 'I'm fine, thank you. You? Can I get you another glass of wine?'

'Oh, yes, I'm very well, thank you. A glass of the blush, if you don't mind.'

Dave returned with two full glasses to find she had busied herself at the food table in his absence. She held a plate containing so many sausage-rolls he worried whether her frail wrist could take the weight. He gave her the glass of wine and took the plate. As he stood sipping and chatting, the elderly woman methodically ate her way through the small mountain of greasy finger food. People had cast disapproving glances in his direction when they had first espied Dave holding the laden plate. When they eventually witnessed the old lady inhaling the food, they came over to express their admiration at the feat. Jones came by and introduced himself and his wife. After putting down his glass and shaking hands with the man, Dave handed him the platter and shook hands with Mrs. Jones. He left the man holding the few remaining sausage rolls.

The worshipper to whom Dave had given the pound coin for the collection plate approached him. 'That was a decent thing you did back there in the church,' the man said as he introduced himself and shook Dave's hand.

'Think nothing of it,' Dave replied.

'I think it would be fair for me to repay you with a tenner,' the man offered and he thrust the money at his benefactor.

'I saw you had to put twenty in the plate, so this tenner should square things up between us.'

Dave was tempted to counter with the sum of thirty-four but he remained silent and stuffed the money in his pocket. 'Thanks.'

Lord Forestbrown was discussing fox hunting with a group of people.

'I don't like the way the fox is killed,' said one, 'but I believe in the right of people to hunt.'

'S'all bloody political,' observed another. 'Labour government trying to prove to their liberal-minded supporters that they haven't gone completely conservative. Now they want to keep the number of foxes down by gassing the poor buggers. Send out some little man in a green smock to pipe cyanide gas down the animals' holes.'

'I saw one report on television that tried to make out fox hunting is an elitist pastime,' a silver-haired lady joined the conversation.

Another weighed in. 'They should come and meet the members of our hunt. We've got a butcher, two carpenters and a second-hand car salesman. Sent the Labour Party a letter about our position but we never heard back from them.'

Mr. Higgins joined the conversation, 'Bloody communists and professional agitators paying gullible students a couple of quid and a sandwich to spend the day protesting. Why doesn't the bloody BBC show them being bussed to the locations and given their instructions for the day? These kids have no idea what they're protesting against.'

'Probably that Jack Straw fellow,' opined another.

'I think he's in the government now, isn't he?'

'Fox hunting should be banned,' thundered a lady who had heard enough. 'It's just an excuse to get drunk and then ride all over the countryside and across people's fields without regard for anyone's property rights.'

'You're right about them getting drunk,' added a young woman. 'I've seen some of them so potted; their horses had a hard job to keep them in the saddle.'

Lady Forestbrown appeared at Dave's elbow. 'Would you like a slice of stohlen?' she offered.

'Thank you.'

'I bought it in Düsseldorf. Apparently, that's *the* place to get it. Supposed to be the best.'

Dave took a bite and powdered sugar fell on his shirtfront. 'It tastes very good,' he declared, 'but I'm no expert on the stuff.'

'Neither am I,' grinned the lady, 'but it does make a good opening line, don't you think?'

~

'Okay, baths for everyone,' announced Ann when they got back to the house. She and the children went up the stairs. Jane poured two glasses of whiskey and handed one to Dave. As he took his first sip of the warming liquid, Malcolm arrived with his mother, Elizabeth and his business partner, James. Dave put down his drink and went out into the rain to help bring in the assorted foods and gifts. Malcolm went up the stairs two at a time to see his wife and children whilst the rest got acquainted.

'So you're the distraction I've heard about,' Elizabeth boomed as she strode up to Dave with her arms wide apart. 'I don't know if they've told you, so I'll advise you right now that I need three.' Three? Dave saw Jane purse her lips in a kiss and touch her forefinger to her right cheek, her left and then the right again. Dave dutifully kissed the lady three times.

'James Murphy,' announced the man as he shook Dave's hand. 'I hear you work at the Coach House in Kensington. I've had a couple of wets in the place but can't say I recall seeing you there.'

'Maybe it was my day off.'

~

The children watched a Christmas special on the television before they all sat down for a supper of kedgeree. Annabel worried that Father Christmas would not know she wasn't at her London home.

'Aren't you worried about having a strange man in your house?' Jane wanted to know.

'Noooo,' grinned Annabel.

'Send any strange men down the hall to my room,' Grandma Elizabeth instructed the assembly.

~

The children went to bed around nine. An hour later, the adults crept up the stairs and brought down gifts that they placed under and around the Christmas tree. After a nightcap or two they too retired for the night.

In the bedroom, Dave produced the package he had hidden from Jane for the last two weeks. He had remembered Edgar's promise of help if he ever needed anything and had asked the antique dealer to find a nice piece of antique jewellery, preferably a ring, for Jane. The man had brought a ring encrusted with diamonds, sapphires and emeralds to Dave. 'It's about two-hundred-and-thirty years old,' he had said. 'I'll sell it to you for the same price I paid an estate for it. It's an incredible bargain.' The ring cost more than Dave had wanted to spend on Jane's Christmas present but as it was a one-time opportunity, he had given Edgar his money and his thanks.

'Merry Christmas, Jane.'

She took the small parcel and started to carefully unwrap it. 'You shouldn't have. Thank you. Wait a minute, of course you should have.' She laughed and her eyes shone with happiness. 'My present to you is under the tree. I'll get it after I've opened this.' When she finally opened the box, she stilled. 'Oh, Dave, this is beautiful. Thank you so much.' She walked into his arms. 'It must have cost a fortune.'

'It did,' he whispered, 'so don't expect me to spend as much at Christmas again. This was a one-off because I love you and because it's our first Christmas together.'

Jane stood back, put the ring on the ring-finger of her left hand and admired it anew. 'So you think we'll have other Christmases together, do you?'

'Yeah, lots of them,' he said.

She suddenly became focused again. 'Oh, your present. I'll be back in a tick.'

She returned with a packaged wrapped in different paper to that used for everyone else's gifts. 'Merry Christmas, Dave.'

He snatched at the ribbon and tore away the paper to find a jewellery box. Inside, he discovered a pair of gold cuff-links with his initials carved on one side. He drew Jane into him. 'Thank you. I shall wear them tomorrow. Now, let's see if we can thank each other very quietly.'

~

Guy awoke Jane and Dave next morning. The boy rapped on every bedroom door and excitedly announced, 'Santa's been. Santa's been.'

Dave looked at his watch and discovered it was eight o'clock. The kids needed a lesson on how to act on Christmas Day. He would have been down the stairs before dawn to make sure presents were under the tree.

After a shower, he descended to the living room to find himself alone. He saw a turkey through the glass door of the oven, so someone had been down before him. He selected a book of short stories from the bookcase and settled in to wait for the chaos.

Elizabeth came down about an hour later. 'Merry Christmas, David. Why aren't my grandchildren opening their presents?'

'Merry Christmas to you. I've no idea. Guy woke us up to tell us Santa had been, and then I think he must have gone back to bed.'

'My son has always been a disciplinarian, but this is a bit much. Those poor children must in their beds, writhing with anticipation. Speaking of writhing, no-one sent any strange men to my room last night.' Dave was at a loss to respond to the statement. The woman had to be in her late sixties or seventies. 'I see that I've appalled you. Don't worry, you'll get used to me.' She turned to the stairs. 'I'm going to rouse Malcolm and Ann. Shall I give Jane a shout as well?'

'If you don't mind. Third door on the right, next to the bathroom.'

~

Fifteen minutes later, Ann appeared, kissed Dave Merry Christmas, and began to make sandwiches from the smoked salmon and brown bread Malcolm had brought with him the night before. She quartered a couple of lemons and placed them on top of the pile. Jane arrived, her hair damp from a shower. She opened a tin of French olives, drained the liquid and poured the contents onto a large serving dish. It was now noon and Dave thought it time to bring out the Amontillado he and Jane had brought with them. The couple toasted each other and ate a couple of the very tasty sandwiches.

Annabel and Guy came down the stairs in their Christmas outfits. The back of Annabel's sweatshirt read 'Innocent until proved guilty'. Guy wore his favourite piece of clothing; a red hooded sweatshirt from The Gap. Dave was utterly surprised when both children, instead of running to inspect the presents under the tree, grabbed a sandwich and started to eat. He was waiting for one or both of them to declare the smoked salmon sandwiches inedible, but they thoroughly enjoyed the food and even picked up a second one. Annabel ate so many olives; both Jane and he had to caution her to slow down.

James and Elizabeth joined the party, stating Malcolm would not be long.

Malcolm entered the room to cries of, 'Daddy, Daddy, Daddy'.

The adults settled into the seats assigned by the children who then acted as 'gift angels'. They picked up presents from under the tree and looked at the labels to see to whom they were addressed. If the name of the recipient was unclear, they took the package to their mother for clarification. Whenever an angel found a gift addressed to them, he or she cried out with delight. If a present was for the other child, it was dutifully, if not happily, added to the correct heap. The children kept an eye on the size of the piles of gifts and Guy muttered more than once that his sister's pile looked bigger than his did. Malcolm lifted the boy onto his lap and explained that some of Annabel's gifts were bulky items and so it looked like she had more, but as often happens in life, good things frequently come in small parcels. Guy gave the matter some thought, and then hastily accepted the argument as he noticed his sister put two more packages on her own pile.

Snow began to fall outside the bay window as the group started to open their gifts. Guy supervised the operation, not wanting to miss seeing what everyone received. It looked to Dave as if the procedure might take a few hours.

Malcolm must have been thinking the same thing. 'You kids carry on opening your presents. Daddy is going to open some champagne.'

'But the tea and coffee are ready now,' his wife protested.

'Fine, dear. You have your tea and I have my champers.'

Malcolm, Elizabeth, Jane and Dave had champagne whilst James asked for coffee and Ann opted for tea. Dave got the impression James would have preferred some bubbly but wanted to show support for his hostess. Dave ate two more sandwiches. Annabel grabbed the champagne cork and added it to her pile of opened gifts.

Blonde and brunette dolls with their high chairs, perambulators, clothes, brushes, mirrors, an iron and an ironing board joined video cassettes, educational toys and assorted confectionery at Annabel's site. Guy amassed a small carpenter's leather belt with the appropriate tools, a potato gun, Star Wars Lego sets, books, videocassettes, and animal slippers. He also received an electric model railway including enough rolling stock to rival Virgin, a model farm with animals the same scale as the railway, and the same confectionery as his sister.

Ann removed labels from wrapping paper and filed them away for the later writing of 'thank you' notes. She stuffed the wrapping paper, cardboard boxes, ribbons, and bows into garbage bags.

'Make sure you get all the instruction manuals, whilst you're about it,' cautioned her husband.

'Yes sir!' she replied as she threw him a mock salute.

~

Dave peeled potatoes whilst James prepared Brussels sprouts and Jane made bread and cranberry sauces.

Guy ran into the kitchen. 'Annie is jumping up and down on one of her dolls,' he advised everyone. The delicious expectation of the trouble brewing for his sister was clearly evident on his young face. Everyone went into the living room to find out what was happening.

'Annabel, why are you jumping on your new doll?' her grandmother wanted to know.

'She won't wee wee,' the child complained a little breathlessly. 'I want her to wee wee.' Her next jump brought her down on top of the doll and she lost her balance, giving Malcolm the opportunity to retrieve the new toy. It was surprisingly unharmed.

'Did you keep the instruction manual for this one?' Malcolm asked his wife.

Ann looked through the drawer where she had put all the items she had earlier saved. 'Here it is,' she announced with some relief.

'Right. Now let's see how to make this blasted doll take a piss.'

'Daddy said a bad word,' Guy gleefully observed.

'Daddy's bad,' his mother told the boy. 'You'll never use a word like that will you darling.'

'Of course he bloody will,' said Elizabeth.

~

Elizabeth stopped the *'Toad of Toad Hall'* video that the children were watching and told them to be quiet for twenty minutes while they all listened to the Queen's speech. The six adults arrayed themselves in front of the television. The children sat on the floor in front of them, each quietly playing with one of their new toys. Malcolm got up from his armchair and opened a bottle of red wine and another of white. The reigning monarch's face appeared and she wished them all a Merry Christmas. She went on to say that youth and technology were not the most important assets of the day, and Dave tuned out.

Bloody Royals, he thought. How can anyone put up with such an idea at the dawn of the second millennium? Come the New Year she'll put out a list of favoured people who are to receive a title or an honour. Dave knew the choices weren't hers, but the idea still rankled. He wondered if 'commoners' were still expected to cheer and kneel. He certainly wouldn't.

Elizabeth stood up when, at the conclusion of the speech, the national anthem was played. Dave remained silent, but he did wonder if she was standing for the Queen, for England or because one of her legs had gone to sleep.

'I see she's giving us another bloody speech on New Year's Day,' James advised.

'Yes, but so is Tony Blair,' Elizabeth said forcefully. 'Just who does he think he is?'

'He's the Prime Minister mum,' said Malcolm, 'and as such he is far more important than the figurehead we just watched.'

'Maybe politically, but he isn't in the same class as Her Majesty the Queen.'

'Hang on Mum,' said Malcolm as he walked over to the clock on the mantel. He opened the face of the timepiece and started to wind back the hands.

'What are you doing?' his mother inquired.

'I'm turning back the clock. If I stand here and do it long enough, I'll get the time back to the age you want it to be.'

'You always were a hateful child.'

Jane found a movie on the television, 'Enough of this. 'Singing in the Rain' is on the box.'

Dave expected a protest from one or both of the children but none was voiced.

Elizabeth brightened 'Oh, I always had a soft spot for Gene Kelly.'

'The scenes with Cyd Charisse will do it for me,' Dave said with a grin. 'She must have the longest legs in the world.'

Guy shot Gene Kelly in the eye with his potato gun.

'Make sure you pick up those potato pellets,' his father warned him.

When the screen showed Kelly swinging in the rain on a lamppost with an umbrella, Jane coughed discretely. Dave looked at her and she pointed at the television. 'Is this our song?' she mouthed. He nodded his head and smiled.

~

They sat down for the traditional turkey dinner at five. There was an assortment of wines on the table and the adults helped themselves to whatever took their fancy. James had carved the turkey and piled the slices of the juicy meat high on an enormous platter. Two kinds of stuffing were in bowls in the middle of the table. Dave was the only one to prefer the dark meat and had no trouble transferring a large portion of it onto his plate. Mashed potatoes, gravy, bread sauce, and cranberry sauce joined the meat. He passed on the sprouts.

An hour later, Malcolm opened a bottle of German dessert wine whilst Ann poured cognac over the plumb pudding and set fire to it.

'Look Daddy. It's blue,' cried Annabel in delight.

'That's because it's cold,' advised her superior-sounding brother.

'No. It's fire, so it's hot,' his sister countered.

'Daddy said that blue means cold,' Guy insisted.

'What I said, young man, was that the blue flame we get from burning the cognac poured over the pud is relative cool. It *is* still hot, however.'

A platter of warm mince pies and an apple pie arrived at the table, together with brandy butter and clotted cream. After they had eaten their fill of the sweet dishes, Ann produced a large stone jar of Stilton and some water biscuits. James made a dramatic production out of slicing off the top of the cheese and a discussion ensued as to whether the creamy substance should be sliced or spooned. Slicing won out and the blue-veined dessert made its way round the table.

Malcolm opened a bottle of port and produced a box of cigars.

'Not in here, please,' begged Ann. 'If you must smoke those things, take them out to the conservatory or, better yet, take a stroll outside with them.'

'Do you know how long it takes to smoke one of these? We'll freeze to death outside.'

'Okay then, use the conservatory.'

The men picked up the cheese, biscuits, port, cognac, plates, knives and linen serviettes and made their way to what Malcolm called 'The Glass House'.

'Come on, you two,' Malcolm ordered the children.

'No, Daddy. It's cold in there,' Annabel protested.

'You'll be sorry,' sang a momentarily musical father.

'Come on Annie,' urged Guy.

They all trooped into the cool room and placed the food and drinks on a wicker table. Malcolm fished in a drawer beneath the tabletop and extracted some sparkler fireworks.

'Sparklers! Sparklers!' Annabel clapped her hands together and jumped around the room.

Malcolm gave one of the fireworks to his son and lit it. Guy held the wire rod in his hand and marvelled at the crackling fire. The glow from the stream of sparks highlighted his massive grin.

'Me too,' Annabel demanded.

'Okay, but you must hold the sparkler just like your brother. Do you understand, Annie?'

'Yes Daddy,' she agreed as she put out her hand to take hold of the unlit firework. Malcolm held the cigarette lighter to the end of the rod until the sparks started to fly. Annabel held on with both hands, stretching her arms out rigidly in front of her. She kept the sparks as far away as possible, a mixture of fear and delight on her face. Each child enjoyed three sparklers before the supply was exhausted.

'More, Daddy,' demanded Annabel as she stamped her foot.

'Don't you stamp your feet at me, young lady,' Malcolm sternly told her.

'It's okay Annie. He'll get some more. Won't you Daddy?'

'For you son? How could I refuse? I'll make sure we have some for New Year's Eve.'

Five minutes later, Jane entered the room to collect the children and take them to the kitchen to see an extra gift Santa had left.

~

Cold forced the rest of them back into the house within forty-five minutes to find the children sat at the dining table, each facing a small furry object.

'Look everybody, this is my 'Flurry',' Guy announced.

Annabel wanted everyone to notice her doll as well. The 'Flurries' talked to the children in an unknown language. Jane consulted a booklet that had accompanied the toys and translated the noises into English. One 'Flurry' announced he was tired and promptly fell asleep. The other was apparently hungry, so Guy let it feed on the tip of his finger.

'Okay. Time for bed,' Ann announced.

'Can I take my 'Flurry' with me?'

'Yes, but he has to sit on your dresser.'

Jane asked for a moment alone with the two toys, during which she read the instruction manual and put the dolls into a 'deep sleep mode'. After a round of hugs and kisses for everyone the children climbed the stairs, taking care not to awaken the 'Flurries'.

~

All adults pitched in with the cleaning up. Elizabeth retrieved stray glasses from various rooms. Jane cleared the tables and wrapped left-over food. Ann put away dishes washed and dried by the men.

When done, Dave helped himself to a lemon sorbet and a glass of water. The others accepted his offer to serve them the same. Malcolm put stoppers on all his open bottles and extinguished the candles.

'Oh, I almost forgot,' Malcolm grinned. 'I have an extra gift for you lot.' He winked at James as he started up the stairs. He returned within a minute with four plastic shopping bags, one of which he handed to everyone except James.

Dave pulled a light-grey sweatshirt from the bag and in doing so caused a quantity of white and green business cards to spill onto the carpet. He dutifully picked up the cards and put them back into the shopping bag. He noticed that the cards were for: 'World Wide Word' – your answer to advertising on the web.' The sweatshirt bore the same green message and, like the cards, gave the reader the address of a web-site www.wwword.co.uk

'I didn't know you were one of those dot-com companies,' Elizabeth said.

'I didn't know you knew what a dot-com company was, mother. Maybe I should wind the hands on that clock forward a little.'

'How could you?' Jane demanded. I bring a guest to your house for Christmas and you try to get him to become a walking sandwich board for your business!'

'Ease up there little sister-in-law. I don't want Dave to become a sandwich board for me. I want all of you to wear the shirt proudly. Any business you put our way will get you a five per cent commission. Cash if you prefer. Offshore bank accounts if you need 'em.' He laughed

'Off-shore bank accounts!' Jane refused to let the matter drop. 'You should be ashamed of yourself.'

'Oh lighten up Jane,' her sister admonished.

Dave put his arm around Jane's shoulder. 'Don't worry about it. We can always turn them inside out.' he grinned.

'Actually, we thought of that,' James laughed. 'The logo is machine stitched into the fabric so it'll just be a whole bunch of green stitching on view if you reverse the garment.'

He had so far worn the sweatshirt only at home. He wrote

Malcolm's details in his diary in case he overheard someone at the bar declare a need for such a service. He considered throwing the business cards away but decided to keep two of them against the day he was required to produce one in front of Jane's family.

Aknowledgements

Hillary Clinton said it takes a village to raise a child. That could also be said for this book. The members of Phoenix House Writers Group have all heard and critiqued some of these chapters and I owe them a debt. (Especially Nicole Hayes, the facilitator, and Sylvia Karakaltsas who both gave me good advice.) My wife has supported me throughout; she was the person who first suggested I pick up a pen. Robert New of Tale Publishing has provided the guidance and service that has put my words into book form. Thank you all.

About the author

Since *Boswell's Fairies*, a tale about recruit training in Her Britannic Majesty's Corps of Royal Marines, was published in 2017, Peter Lingard has turned his style of writing to tell of life in an English public house. Peter worked in a London pub for a while (although it was nothing like the one depicted here) and thereby gained the experience necessary to write this book. These days he prefers wine to beer, but his love of Manchester City FC is constant.

www.ingramcontent.com/pod-product-compliance
Ingram Content Group UK Ltd.
Pitfield, Milton Keynes, MK11 3LW, UK
UKHW041830200726
13854UKWH00002BA/914